The Strike

In Praise of The Strike

The Strike lies somewhere near the tradition of Ulysses or Mrs Dalloway. Thomlinson's prose feels purposeful and sharp, even as it explores illusory, shifting emotions. The novel's pyrotechnic language serves primarily as a window into the minds of his characters, resulting in a book where characterization and aesthetics are inseparable.

— LA Review of Books

Like that of Gertrude Stein, the writing in Thomlinson's The Strike ruptures ordinary syntax to create a jarring reading experience that in Thomlinson's case, mirrors the backdrop of political upheaval for its characters. What emerges in Thomlinson's tapestry—is a compelling narrative inextricably connected to its creative telling, replete with a beautiful, poetic layer woven into the experimental syntax.

— Krysia Jopek, author of Maps and Shadows and Hourglass Studies

Thomlinson, though, takes a more fluid approach, weaving together the external and internal in a single sentence. Not only are the descriptions vivid, but they demonstrate how memories and observations often bleed into one another. Thomlinson skillfully uses sensory details to pinpoint sensations that are difficult to capture in ordinary language.

— Kate Findley – author of Demented Fairytales

This unconventional text while reminiscent of the Dadaists word games, experimental poetry, and William Burroughs's work using cut-ups is, in the end, a unique entity unto itself. Don't expect traditional sentence structure or punctuation. A challenging but satisfying novel for those looking for something at the very cutting edge of different.

— Ray Fracalossy – author of Tales from the Vinegar Wasteland

The Strike

by Harvey Thomlinson

LucidPlay
Publications

The Strike

Lucid Play Publishing,
3322B King Street,
Berkeley, California 94703,
USA.

Chapter One was first published as Old Yu Writes Words in Tears on the Fence (Nov. 2011.)

Early versions of Chapters Three and Eleven were first published in Exclusive Magazine (2013).

Bensko's interview with the author first appeared on the Experimental Writing website in 2018.

Cover design by Mandy Wang

ISBN 978-069-29994-4-8

The subject that I am is inseperable from this body and this world.
— *Merleau-Ponty. Phenomenology of Perception.*

Contents

Oh Bondage. Up yours!
一 *Poly Styrene. X-Ray Specs.*

Harvey Thomlinson is best known as a translator of contemporary Chinese fiction, including novels by Murong Xuecun and Chen Xiwo. His translations have appeared in *The New York Times* and *The Guardian*, and his translation of Murong's *Leave Me Alone* was longlisted for the MAN International Literary Prize. His own innovative writing has circulated through small-press and independent journals such as *Exclusive Magazine* (US) and *Tears on the Fence* (UK). His long-term work-in-progress, *The Sentence*, will be published by Lucid Play in 2019. He also runs Make-Do Publishing, a small press specialising in fiction from Asia.

The Strike

1

Mrs Zhang was depressed purple leaves scattered along austere avenue because the wind was strong few of her friends were in the park. She came here every morning although this winter was severe her exercises required suffering. Walking with her bag of vegetables east of the crematorium there was always a wilderness.

All the chat of their park regulars that morning by the rusted pagoda turned around the strike. Mrs Liu had heard from her nephew at the Bright Moon plant they bent and stretched. A bird started amid winter foliage Mrs Zhang felt edgy remembering long ago violence by their frozen river.

According to Mrs Liu as the earth moved round the sun Bright Moon workers had marched to People's Square.

Later Mrs Zhang climbed seven flights of stairs to warn her husband of many decades Old Yu in the kitchen the television leaked its dull gleam. After moving to this new apartment two years ago light squibs blasting weakly from the balcony festival ribbons still fluttered.

Old Yu have you heard about Bright Moon?

These days she didn't know whether he heard things supping soup noodles in their small kitchen they lived often as not. She studied his tired face for answers their daughter long gone dust thick on the plants.

Don't tell me you're still going to the river?

She thought it might be risky now as he rinsed his bowl in the icy courtyard just like years ago. By watching him she knew he'd suffered slipping on his long thin coat gathering his foam tipped brush until she was scared he'd disappear.

Take care, Old Yu.

He was Old Yu with his waterbrush and felt coat since forever. So far there were no signs flat grey windows timber factory road several buses trundling by he didn't wish to stop them. He just walked on slow men in long coats scraping ice off the road with small bundles of sticks.

Old Yu lowered his bucket through one of the holes in the black ice his long lost love's eyes.

Good rain knows the time of the seasons

Thirty years had gone by since his dear friend Guihua's disappearance the river freezing over for months. He still often thought about that summer the soldiers came her banners flying high in the sky dirty lumps of ice. One night floating half submerged below a bridge they saw bodies on their way home from the factory the army took her.

Squatting on a page of last week's Suifen Times he poked his brush in the bucket her startled mouth paper soft under his knees ink smell rising then wiped gently around the edges. With the wet brush he stroked the shapes of words on the frozen ground hard and cold as a traitor's heart.

Just when spring comes it appears

Since his father taught him as a youngster to write words the rhythm of that hand still in his own until now he came to the river alone. He let the brush fly lightly above the ground a menacing atmosphere collecting in thin lines and thick.

Stealing into the night with the wind

Often kids watched as he guided his brush curving and darting across the frozen earth. Somehow he sensed a different music today echoes thick with warning.

Clouds above the wild path all dark

River mist flooded along the embankment footsteps. He stayed

2

there writing his words by the water his stiff back locked in ancient ice. The first few words faded already a shadow lengthening before his former colleague came into sight.

Old Yu, have you heard?

For more than a decade Old Yu was Young Zhou's boss at the timber works tall wire fences still ringing deep yards like memory. After the works were shuttered six years back Young Zhou joined his father at the Bright Moon electricity plant the air smelled of sulfur.

Something's going down at Bright Moon.

Approaching middle age Young Zhou looked like his father Anguo union man at Bright Moon under dirty clouds stacking to heaven. Anguo was sick he'd heard the brush moving over the ground. Many of his generation had dropped dead in the last few years they sometimes met now in the new supermarket. Angry murmurs carried in the still air dipping his brush.

Young Zhou studied him beneath a weak sun he squatted with his brush drops of water. You see he said we need you to write words for our banner before they crush us

Old Yu wished he would get lost.

We won't lie down and let those dogs sell the plant Young Zhou declared

a match flared.

You're the only one who can help us comrade

pressing the old buttons

Old Yu was reluctant for some time Young Zhou insisted no one better to write the banner

a small bird lay stiff in the snow.

Eventually he agreed to come even dead

the creature still looked hungry.

We need you, Old Yu.

He was Zhou Junjie leading his former boss Old Yu back to town the night before it had snowed heavily. With Father under police guard in the hospital he was dead afraid word spreading through dusk

3

neighbours appearing.

He left his wife Jiaying in their bedroom face to the wall going from the electricity estate onto Zhongshan Road.

They say the crowds are huge like thirty years ago he warned Old Yu the road slippery.

With the Bright Moon estate still after the night blizzard neighbours emerged in ones and twos from concrete stairwells strung with garlic bulbs. The banner union deputy Mrs Gao said to their comrades reaching the bridge a weak sun penetrated through the mist we must find a writer of words. Several of them suggested Old Yu because the street lights still on he was well known in their town for his brushwork.

I've heard about those bad old days, Old Yu.

Car horns blasting wind wailing.

They reached the crowd on the bridge the lights were off now. Junjie felt nervous his father wasn't there to decide what would happen next this cold morning sweat pricking his back within layers of clothes.

Old Yu, it's Old Yu.

He was Old Yu as they swept him towards Mrs Gao with her pot and long sheets of paper stretched out on the grimy ice slabs of the bridge.

We can't let them sell our factory Mrs Gao said job losses were feared

the sun rose a little at a time. They will steal our children's future she warned him

under the factory grey sky.

There's people going hungry.

They pushed the ink brush into Old Yu's hand as he knelt on the paper walling him in with their long coats and caps. Some hugged themselves to keep warm a donkey cart trotting by.

Sirens

We're counting on you, Old Yu.

The Strike

Engines.

Old Yu's weathered hand scratched across the paper the words they told him that morning. His back felt sore squatting in the dim early light near the ground Gao Lihua and he had worked side by side a lifetime ago. He feared he might not be able to stand again as a young man she knew the mistakes that bent his heart.

You haven't lost your touch, Old Yu.

Still the crowd grew he shut them from his mind shouting slogans so they wouldn't see his hand shaking on Zhongshan Bridge legs numb beneath him. Smokers scattered ash in gusts of wind over the paper words of encouragement.

Old Yu is a real hero.

Although they jolted his arm with all his force he inscribed the banner like thirty years ago during the troubles sky pressing lower in the air a scent of iron. When for Guihua and her gang he wrote hold high the banner of revolution at the machine factory ink watery. Her rebel sisters praised his posters excitedly posting them on trees and walls several times he went over each brush stroke.

We are the future now.

With one last stroke he finished a cheer going up Mrs Gao holding the banner high many hands grabbing for it.

Our wives ask for our salary, our children ask for education, our parents ask for medical treatment.

She was Mrs Gao now her children out of work the past a poisoned legacy. Their town was once an industrial furnace but young people rotted as coal fires smudged earth and sun. She and Old Yu knew about suffering the expression went how low the sky hung over them. While they'd talked only a few times compared with the old days his brush strokes seeming emotional she guessed he'd paid for hi

Your words are good as ever, Old Yu.

He seemed content as the banner waved through the air they moved onward in a surge of bodies and breath. Young Zhou leading the crowd spread at last flowing from the bridge. Soon they were going past newspaper vendors a mass of clothed winter bodies inside small plastic huts with smoking chimneys.

We demand to see the mayor.

In this moment he was Zhou Junjie finally the town speaking up as they went by small shops with strange letters along Vladivostok Road. Although the whole world seemed to be drifting through space Little Wei his wife hadn't shown up for weeks waging a cold war. Since she appeared bored of him they seldom made love in their small apartment little space for intimacy.

Old Yu, what can they do against so many of us?

He was Old Yu as time advanced strange hope in his heart at the emergence of so many people after all these years. Since he and his wife got married during exile in the countryside their once rich town had died while the future passed them by. Winter mornings he often took his daughter to the timber work baths still in his mind until a great shout went up behind him.

We demand justice.

The march proceeded down Zhongshan Road that wild night thirty years ago the army everywhere. We know Miss Xia influenced you the mean captain from Hebin said passing the Northern Bank with her family background.

The day before at the factory gates they waved goodbye as the march trudged on a scrawny cat mewing in the snow.

Workers were all through the faint distant sun with their dense bodies as they approached People's Square in the middle of February. Since the town government started selling off the factories one by one discontent deepened until the Bright Moon workers reached the gates of City Hall. Some of them hadn't been paid for a year in the frosty air south of the border.

Your banner is flying real proud, Old Yu.

Seeing the red dragon soar above the crowd his eyes damp with tears clouds stacked above the earth. At last their town was standing up again although the gates of City Hall remained closed their voices rang out without reply. After meeting at the commune thirty years ago he and Jiahui were wed in their army uniforms a small flask of snake wine was passed through the crowd. Without warning the snake burning bitter in his mind he saw Guihua the day after her arrest the victorious faction parading her in a dunce's hat. As she knelt on a workshop bench they read aloud the statement he'd already written at their command the wine hitting him. Their fists waved above him ink splattering he broke away

the crowd's roar thinning into wind.

Old Yu, comrade, where are you going?

He was Old Yu elbows flying suddenly his mind slipping the ground was icy. While his banner flew in the sky they waited for the gates to open that afternoon something would happen.

Old Yu!

At first he wasn't sure where to run this morning itself seemed to curse his name although he knew the back alleys. This was where he'd spent his whole life a woman in red waited at the underground steps her breath white. There'd been many changes since his child was young Suifen still lagged behind thick plastic curtains to keep out the biting wind

Old Yu.

The Border Police Bureau occupied a gray stone building on the corner of Liberation Street and Station Road a uneasy sound roaring in his ears. While the years opened and shut, he would never forget how the thuggish captain found him that night swans over grey sky.

We're giving you one chance to save yourself.

Stumbling past the hospital ever since returning from exile he'd tried to live quietly in their small apartment built on land once owned by the timber works. Weekday mornings going out with brush and bucket to write his words on the embankment making ritual family visits.

She's the poisonous snake we want.

The Strike

Suddenly he knew his past had caught up with him without much resistance his legs strode through time and space. Whatever happened today at City Hall street cobblers squatting in the spring morning he faced an overdue reckoning.

You're not really the hero type.

Without intending it he'd arrived at the old station theatre as the matinee had already started the steps slippery. Just as if it was a normal Tuesday Old Yu went up the dirty concrete staircase stars smiled blankly into the theatre dust drifted.

Slowly old men sat in the light from high curtains small chairs smoking as the show went on. Scattering ash throughout the early afternoon blue retired overalls the audience drank tea low wood tables amid ripped red seats.

Old Yu, friend, this isn't your usual day.

He sat down among them as if today was really ordinary cream yellow curtains hanging thickly down the dusty air. While time unfurled rumours about the strike a woman with a red corset on a stool while a stage comic with a false beard sang.

Show me the way to the sea dragon's cave.

All around the hall murmurs spread on Yanan Road hundreds while tea waitress Xu Yue stumbled round the theatre band starting up. Slow dust light on their faces the mayor's been beaten up as they passed the time since the jobs started disappearing one by one
they turned to him.

That Mayor Ma has been dismissed, did you hear, Old Yu?

No, I haven't heard.

The red corset pulled the comic down on a mat Old Yu denying everything around him voices rising with the news laughter spilling through the hall. While the performance rattled on raucously his mind drifted to scenes he hadn't thought about so much recently.

I don't know anything about it.

Guihua's face numb with horror years ago the comic and the corset feigning embraces as everyone in the yard shouted denunciations. Although he longed to intervene hadn't they warned him of the consequences if he stepped out of line the song clanging as memory broke open.

Down with the poisonous snakes and demons.

The way they hacked off Guihua's long hair that afternoon the theatre stank of damp and smoke. In his mind he felt flickering hope of forgiveness as the comic stood up and started to sing a song about the emperor. Surely his terrible mistake had been a longlongtimeago cigarette ash dropping through sunrays into the chairs.

She had glanced at him despairingly throat dry as dust he thought the comic dropping his trousers as they dragged her away.

Old Yu, there's a cop looking for you.

Xu Yue the young person who served tea was there due to the midget's backside laughter sweeping the hall.

She said you better come quickly Old Yu as the audience applauded

chair scraping.

Your brush, Old Yu.

Grasping his brush for security Old Yu went to the back of the hall the comic singing a subversive poem in a reedy voice a few people looked around. Officer Zhang Gang waited in the doorway afternoon pale around him.

We need to talk, old friend.

They entered the theatre office painfully thin Xu Yue still pushed her trolley with tea urn and glasses. Zhang Gang showed Old Yu a chair while Little Xu was made to leave there looking at the peeling theatre posters on the walls.

What's this we've heard about you provoking trouble.

In the light of day Zhang Gang's expression was tough the midget's song carried from the hall and suggested no tolerance. Inciting social disorder was a serious offence as he of all people should know his heart raced dangerously.

I didn't mean anything.

The Strike

Zhang Gang asked him what his wife would say within thick smoke Little Xu listening.

He was Old Yu as the past continued following Officer Zhang down the staircase and into the afternoon.

The Strike

2

He was Chen Yun after his train stopped moving deliberately dark clouds smoked above the platform. Soldiers grimly patrolled the station with pistols he hadn't eaten for hours.

Where have you come from?

The soldiers demanded to see his ticket in weird panic heart leaping dangerously he feared it was lost. He held his nerve with great effort producing the stub they waved him on into the knife cold grimy square.

There just as his union boss Old Wang had described was the solid stone frontage of the Northeastern Hotel choked by the night army trucks stalled outside. Old Wang had reckoned he'd be safe at the hotel soldiers swooping everywhere until he'd made contact with a certain union man at the Bright Moon plant.

Chen Yun was unsure what to do in a clandestine corner of the square a taxi driver was handing around smokes to others. As he listened to their chat stealthily a truck began to trundle in their direction a gust of wind brought new revelations:

Bright Moon workers in People's Square. That bastard mayor's been locked up.

It seemed from these words the troubles had spread faster than Old Wang predicted the temperature dropping. On the lower bunk of the green train that afternoon a band of timber workers had mentioned the new wave of arrests yesterday in his home town drinking and carpeting the floor with sunflower shells. The danger had caught up with him although he'd just arrived cigarettes sparked feebly in the night.

Since the Northeastern Hotel seemed too risky for him now Chen Yun walked on into the future. Opposite in the hotel he saw lights mysterious and welcoming as the streets were frozen black with winter.

All along the station road were hole in the wall cafes with thick plastic curtains over their doors to keep out the cold his stomach rumbled emptily. The dark swirled in around waiters bearing soup noodles and pork dumplings he felt sick at the thought of what he'd left behind.

The day their comrades were brought up grayblack dead from the flooded pit a scrawny cat scratched its behind on a low gray wall. As Old Wang's second in command back home he'd led their fight that summer frequent violent thunder storms.

For the first time since his wife left him during the troubles he felt calm although he'd never been here before this borderland was where he belonged. He'd got away just in time as they'd probably arrested his chief Old Wang that morning metal shutters down all along the street there would be an alert for him. Slipping out before dawn stained sky he never realised the crackdown had started until hearing the conversation on the train the gutters were deep.

A long time ago he'd grown up in a small town like this there was little to be gained from walking all night. As the moon drifted through space he passed many quiet hotels set up high from the street. The fourth or fifth he entered a tired looking woman stood up behind reception no point in going further.

Welcome brother.

She steadily completed the registration form in her early middle age a small room with a bed behind reception. While she examined his fake identity card he glimpsed skin beneath a pile of sheets the lobby smelling of musty decay

You'll find someone up there.

After he dared to ask while giving him the key to 305 she admitted there was talk of trouble at Bright Moon electricity plant.

Apparently it was nothing to do with her lank unswept hair as he went on up the stairs.

The third floor attendant had turned on the third floor landing light and was waiting two mosquitoes flitted by her desk. A big bunch of keys swelled her hand soundlessly mosquitoes unlocking the door to room 305. She stood aside twin beds and a sparsely decorated old television amid emptiness he had a quick look.

Okay?

A minute later she returned with a flask of warm water because the day wasn't over he was still in his shoes. She bent frowningly to lay the flask down under cotton sleepwear her self no longer quite young. It seemed that she wouldn't leave for a long time the flask had a cracked lid.

Anything else?

Sooner than he feared she left like his wife and daughter water pipes murmured three months ago. After his wife threw him out back in the summer a bathroom tap leaked without stopping he went crazy. She'd started resenting him because of the strike he spent most nights with his union comrades encouraging them to stand firm the water heater rumbling. In a daze he stared at the dusty twin bedside tables and the clock until his head started to spin alone still apart from a cockroach.

A cockroach with their dark little plates and wings or were there two of them. They appeared and reappeared mysteriously on the edge of the desk he sat and watched for evidence. At times he saw one on the floor closer really when looking to the curtains it seemed to know he was watching.

Was it truly likely he felt sick a single cockroach could cover so much distance going out into the corridor.

Is anyone there?

Out in the corridor he was Chen Yun as time seeped slowly the lights were off in her room. She'd vanished on a chair sat a pile of dirty sheets until a glow came up behind a door. Only just in time they returned together to room 305 while he demanded a change a massive cockroach crawled across the blue bed sheet. With a silence of complicity they stood side by side watching juicy little wings the way it went slowly on

It's not acceptable.

She agreed to a change that night the atmosphere screamed her indifference. While she helped him carry his bags up to the fourth floor void no indication she found his request reasonable. On the stairs she looked different from behind after unlocking the door to room 409 television bed and desks waited as before.

Will you be alright?

Since her face was blank water running through a pipe he couldn't guess whether she'd been alone in her room. She didn't say anything else just watched him until he waved her away it felt she might stay all night.

Afterwards he sank gloomy carpet scorched with smoke into a pit from which no escape. Wherever he went faded walls there was nowhere to go he thought some time later later the black telephone bleeped.

He didn't know what to do as soft rings persisted more of a vibration reaching for the receiver.

Good evening mister.

A woman's low insidious voice somewhere in the whispering night he wondered if it might actually be a boy. He asked this person in the bathroom the tap leaking where they called from.

This is Jade Heaven, mister.

This night was endless walls for whatever reason silence grew. A moment later broke a burst of female laughter in the background he felt unsettled from the window night creeping in.

I don't want anything, OK?

He dropped the receiver because it was winter the sheets were dead cold. Unseen dangers threatened him from all sides he tried to imagine the caller's face. Minutes passed on the stairs footsteps before he forced himself to focus on a pressing proposition. Because of the arrests back home in a dark place behind the curtains the police would be after him.

He needed news about the situation at Bright Moon was the sullen third floor aunty wandering corridors aimlessly. After he had the facts he could decide whether listening at doors to seek Old Wang's union comrade.

The dead moon drifting through space he turned on the television. He would try calling back home after checking out in the morning a comic with a wispy beard singing for information. To call from this hotel would be mad even if Old Wang hadn't been arrested yet a midget with a blue painted face shaking a staff.

True lovers shall meet on the peony pavilion.

He urged himself to act cautiously although never a strength it might be safest to lie low. We'll rouse this whole land Old Wang said a few days ago he was delusional.

By now he wasn't sure whether he'd really made this doomed journey as Old Wang's errand runner or for his own escapist reasons needing food. As he read the room service menu the telephone rang abruptly his stomach made a growl.

Mister, this is Jade Heaven.

He couldn't remember after a while whether or not he had spoken during the long silence the television whining.

Where is Jade Heaven?

The same faint teasing voice as before said he or she could come to his room above the groan of the heater the night continuing.

When?

The voice whispered from somewhere in the universe she or he would come soon. This creepy stranger might just like him be sat silently watching a still door handle second after second sirens wailing below.

What about the floor aunty?

Several minutes passed nervously he lay down until there were two soft knocks on the door. When he opened a young person stood in the silent corridor for ages shadows spreading across the carpet.

Hello mister.

She slipped past him elusively the door closed with a sweet cloying scent. The stranger went straight to the lamp and dimmed it a few seconds later the sirens fading. Her face looked red sleeveless top and tight black jeans silence apparently newly arrived from some poor village. Chen Yun watched nervously what time it was now the thick tobacco brown curtains drawn.

I'm from Jade Heaven.

Why the hell had he allowed her here from adjacent rooms seeping a sleepless murmur. His body trembled subtly hands reached forward until they touched his shoulders.

Want to relax?

This woman looked kind bold lipstick pout a groaning floorboard reminding him of a waitress he was friends with in a restaurant back home. Her teeth were bad but there was something touching about her bare bony shoulders dust and shadows. They were alone at this point of space and time looking at him almost expectantly something the board creaked again.

Where's Jade Heaven?

She massaged his shoulders warm breath from out of the unseen the water pipes mutedly whistling. He thought her soft but firm touch would mark him so that one day flesh fragrance the moon knew.

Upstairs. Where are you from, handsome?

Without waiting for his answer she said she would go into the bathroom for a moment

Chen Yun half hoped she would just leave.

Chen Yun heard the fan's whine as he stretched out on the bed mingled with a gentle hiss into the toilet bowl. Stale smells rose inside his shirt he had to find someone who knew the situation at Bright Moon.

You are tired?

She was back lifting her red top above his head the ceiling had a discoloured patch. Chen Yun felt nervous again seeing her pale dusty skin and the moonlight and shadows inside he really wanted to talk.

Where are you from?

Her fingers felt strong as Chen Yun lay on his stomach his heart beating faster. She sat casually on his legs after nimbly removing her jeans the measured softness of her touch was like that of a sister.

You come far?

Suddenly Chen Yun feared her visit was a trap because of his rough hands the young woman asked if he was a miner. He felt alarmed that she had guessed so fast apparently he'd revealed too much for comfort loosening his belt

I'm trying to find an old comrade.

What comrade she asked him delicately adjusting her legs as she dug into pooling shadows from behind.

Her legs gripped tight on either side of his stocky trunk

bony pressure. He almost blurted out the name just in time saying a comrade at the window

dust stirred.

She knew the plant apparently because her uncle worked there

probing soreness around his spine.

She talked for a while about staying with her uncle after she first came to the city

his spine sounded crunchy.

Where could he meet Bright Moon comrades Chen Yun asked sensitively

her hands stroking his sides.

It was careless of him to lose his friend's number she said in a mocking tone

loosening his shirt wouldn't this be easier if he turned over.

The Strike

You're strong.

She rolled him over on his back at last the television gone blank.
Her chest was pinched high within the upper shadows of the room his
heart jumped.

You ever been to Suifen before she asked in a murmur
his impressions of the city.

There are attractions to visit like the wartime base she told him
thousands slaughtered there years ago.

Yeah Chen Yun agreed history was shit whatever happened then
he couldn't leave.

The soft curve of her shoulders reminded him of being a young
fool in love during military training in the frozen northern plains.

She moved down from the shadows no way out in unmeasured
time Chen Yun fumbling lost. As they embraced imagining the
watchful floor aunty at the door guilt subdued him. After his failure
she lay there wordlessly touching him the moment ebbing away.
Hands drifting beneath the blanket curiously her warm legs.

The stranger was all flesh and blood trapped inside the frayed blue
blanket the scent of their fleeting intimacy.

You want to see me again?

When Chen Yun asked cautiously his visitor said she could take
him to her uncle's house this weekend
tiredness catching up with her.

She laughed that she might take him there only if he was good to
her
blanket dropping on the floor.

Before midday her phone would be turned off because it was
Saturday
the Jade Heaven ladies slept late.

You give me it now, OK?

The stranger pulled on her red top as Chen Yun offered a red note
mysteriously the soundless television flickering back on. Accepting it

casually she went to the door tomorrow he could call him as the silent images unfolded.

After the door closed Chen Yun listened to footsteps descending secrets in the dark. He thought there were voices although he wasn't sure the cars never stopped on the road outside.

He was Chen Yun came and went. She was back in Jade Heaven right now laughing about him along with her friends wondering where heaven was.

3

She was Xu Yue lay on her side to stay asleep the sheets crawled up her thighs a day yet to penetrate. When her eyes opened she couldn't breathe sometimes they turned up the heating so high chairs with spaces inbetween.

Across the morning her legs stretched remotely sensations stirring last night's clothes piled on the bed. Because it was Saturday no hurry to move a dirty bowl on the floor unless she wanted to. She stayed there languorously loving the soft pillow in her mind dusty light sparkled like emotions.

Time pressed these dim paint walls flat as thoughts a dead moth. Across the scratched old dresser she saw emptied out shit from her bag at the same time her roommate seldom around.

After a while she stood up and stretched with faint hope the gap in the red curtains letting in the pale sun.

The light shimmied throughout the twenty-third floor she remembered her client last night at the Northeastern Hotel. After rejoining the girls at Jade Heaven they all finished a bottle of snake wine laughing at her tale of the stranger's little difficulty the night flew by.

Her window surveyed a misty sea of winter-weathered apartment blocks half a galaxy from her village she lit a first cigarette. For a few moments she tried to imagine her damp family home this morning a cat stalking across cabbages on winter frost roofs.

She'd suffered so much in the city she thought the sky was pregnant with snow. During her early months she worked as a hostess

The Strike

in the Happiness Bar on Xiamen Road the first cigarette of a morning almost made her retch. She played dice with the male customers although their lewdness paid the other hostesses resented her popularity.

Things were more friendly at the Jade Heaven massage center swapping stories over green bottles of beer the manager sent up by midnight the party usually in full swing. Most of the older Jade Heaven crew were married with quaint hairstyles their partners didn't care as long as the money came home.

On busy nights she had to fight with her sisters for mirror space in the bathroom powder clouds swirling. Whatever people said she was a mostly good hearted cute person who deserved better love often came when you least expected it.

She entered the kitchen to heat soy milk the dirty apartment needed cleaning. Her tired fingers took two matches igniting the gas ring a fart sent sparks floating pleasurably through her. There were no clean bowls she remembered she would meet her best friend Yu Wen that afternoon at the Zhongyou Mall

Xu Yue greatly envied Yu Wen a receptionist at the four star Modern Hotel taking her hot soy milk to the bathroom there were even occasional foreign guests. As she sat on the toilet mouth gaping she thought her life would be happier if she could speak other languages like her friend her cellphone rang.

Scampering across the twentythird floor uneven tiles barefoot Xu Yue wasn't sure whether she could make it. She reached her phone just in time sinking onto the dusty sofa their closet mirror showed a bird's nest of hair.

You didn't forget me, did you?

Strange how she'd just been thinking about this man from last night there was a strange atmosphere on the fourth floor of the Northeastern hotel. Winey weariness often erased the early parts of evenings in corners cobwebs accumulated.

You still remember me?

The Strike

Sometimes it happened like this on a balcony opposite a man called during the daytime dry yellow plants. So early the client was like a ghost reaching through darkness she sat there white t-shirt with a slight headache. Sure she remembered giving her number although this was a rest day their manager asked them to cultivate regulars.

She wasn't really listening to him at that moment a woman hanging washing on the balcony last night slipping into the void.

You said you could help me find my comrade at Bright Moon.

Although the day had hardly started grey clothes fallen on the metal railings below she didn't want this person coming to her place later there would be a coating of dust. She had an afternoon shopping date with Yu Wen to plan and the neighbour opposite almost lived on her balcony.

You should keep your word.

Even though there was plenty of time before meeting Yu Wen at Zhongyou she wouldn't tidy for any creep. Of course she shouldn't forget the money her brain was working now which would be useful for many reasons.

We can drink tea this afternoon on Yanan Road, OK?

Naturally she hadn't believed his story about having a friend at the Bright Moon plant men would say any bullshit to get what they wanted. She explained where they should meet later perhaps she'd see how things went.

She stood under the shower the day had a shape when she washed her hair a spider scuttled out. Somehow though all the shopping and stuff she had to do floated up in her mind the spider disappeared down the drain.

Down to her last somewhat clean shirt Xu Yue hoped that she could get rid of this stranger as quickly as possible another week had passed. Saturdays were freer because she didn't have that second job serving tea at the station theater like most afternoons she put on blue jeans and a black sweater. The theatre job hardly paid at all but she took it to soothe that daytime empty feeling her actor friend Chunsheng a player there.

Handsome Chunsheng stamped around the dusty boards three times a day drawing delight from laid-off workers. The audience adored his fooling about on stage thinking nothing of dropping his pants. Chunsheng had taught Xu Yue a few tricks back in the village where they'd both grown up feelings of love deepening. Although Chunsheng stripped for laughs when drunk he was in an intense relationship with A Mi his stage partner. A Mi was crazy and thin like a jumping stick of wood such arrangements usual in the entertainment business.

After Xu Yue was fired by the Happiness Bar from the kindness of his heart Chunsheng helped her to land the gig at Jade Heaven.

She sighed at the tragedy of loving someone stubbing a cigarette she wasn't meant to be with. Her cigarette smouldering no delusion about special talent like those beauties that sold cosmetics in department stores. She had none at all apart from perhaps a small one smiling to make both men and women like her.

She went out as ever elevator operator Aunty Zhu reading a book as she rode up and down her grim face full of years ago. All night and day Aunty perched on a stool beneath the elevator's small electric heater always polite to Xu Yue while probably telling tales about her. Aunty Zhu was married to the head of the residential committee because she knew all the neighbours in the building Xu Yue feared her greatly. With her hair pinned in a scraggly bun Aunty Zhu saw everything riding through the dark night of history to pass time supermarket adverts pasted on the walls.

A few children kicked a ball around the middle of the day it was colder than Xu Yue realised. So far it had been a mild winter seeing old Mr Zhang reading in his small stairwell kiosk she bought cigarettes. Spontaneously she decided to walk one stop outside the apartment yard workers tugged at a rope vanishing underground.

After eight months surviving in this small city as she lit her second cigarette this day mist swirled with her feelings of joy and despair. Joy was the blurred landscape of scraped high rises she inhaled in the white sky. Despair was the memory of how her birth mother gave her away twenty years ago she exhaled in the county hospital. That day her mother's heart was set on a boy as the women in the next bed wanted a girl the light was hidden.

Cautiously she felt her way around trenches of snow rather than disappear this was reinvention. For all that her adoptive parents were kind she couldn't help asking whether the bus really came down this road. She supposed if she'd been a more charming baby bricks poking through snow no sign of it. She wondered what it would be like to have a mother who loved her more than anything the weather perhaps a factor.

The bus slowly approached at age twenty wondering why her friend Wen seemed so confident with strangers while she was a nobody.

Snow was trodden hard on the bus floor as she got on a few elderly women returning from the market with leeks and eggplants stared at her. She was fascinated by city people and liked to learn about their different lives while dreaming about having one of her own.

They were stuck in traffic on the seats behind Xu Yue a young gang in long grey coats talked about the strike at the Bright Moon plant. She wasn't sure what was happening at the yard where her uncle worked hell blaring horns.

They say the mayor's been taken away.

She believed despite the bad traffic it was dangerous to get involved in other people's business. Her Jade Heaven sisters had whispered about the trouble last night between calls rubbing the frosted window with her sleeve.

Who knows what the hell might happen.

There was something strange halfway down Zhongshan Road the moon still visible as memory. Three or four army lorries were parked in a snowy roadside glade soldiers sat on the ground. The lorries had strange number places with fierce round faces the soldiers looked like southerners. They were eating rice out of paper boxes new platoons had arrived overnight the bus air almost thick enough to touch.

Happy Future.

The Happy Future Mall was where she got off a flock of crows darkened the sky on her first visit this new emporium had awed her. She sensed a special atmosphere today the crows landed on the roof of the door portico.

Her stop was outside the store just south of the corner of Yanan and Zhongshan roads twenty police waited under the closed sky. The window dummies stared blankly her mind racing as unpredictable forces threatened this city. Yanan Road was sealed to cars while cops directed traffic with their radios for now she hurried on.

Most of the windows were shuttered from a corner of her eye she saw the lurid sign of the Pink Lipstick cafe. The cafe was open luckily after going in she spotted him at a corner table straight away the music creating a different feeling.

You came.

She became a little shy again approaching him in the cold light of day music seeming familiar. Whenever meeting a client away from the hotel she glimpsed a cockroach scuttling across the mopped floor.

I thought you wouldn't.

In a past life Xu Yue worked at a coaching inn the hostesses sang and danced for their lives. The landlord made enemies one day an outlaw band came to town and chopped all they could find. Too scared to escape broken glass everywhere Xu Yue was tossed in a large barrel of wine the girls drowned no one bothering to pull them out.

This is for you.

The Strike

4

She was Mrs Zhang called her friend Pan Meizhu from their exercise group this stormy night help needed to spring Old Yu from jail. Controversial but rich entrepreneur Meizhu lived with the police chief's brother although they'd never married outside the wind howled.

He didn't mean to get involved in trouble.

She was Meizhu dining with a silk merchant all day she'd heard alarming reports about what was happening at Bright Moon. As a boss she was quick to make decisions waitresses in red tunics scurrying past their table with dishes of lamb slices and pig brain. While she didn't like to bother her powerful sister in law yet again the electric lights in the restaurant flickered.

Where the hell are you going?

Her supplier Dong Hongqi was shameless about his desire to bed her again red lanterns hung low above their heads the night listening in. They'd shared a fling during her southern buying tour last summer the electricity came back on.

She smiled and said she had to call someone with a frown he refilled his glass.

You make me too damn hot.

The revolving lobby doors of the Boiling Point hotpot restaurant spun in the chill north wind Meizhu made her call to police chief Linfeng at home. She was actually desperate to find out from her sister in law what had happened since morning tied up with supplier Dong's silks.

The Strike

As Linfeng's home phone kept ringing she paced restlessly Old Wen
owner of the Zhongyou Mall entering the lobby. The Boiling Point
was popular with big shots from their town dead leaves fluttered in
the revolving door no one cared how you'd made your money.

Haven't eaten yet, Old Wen?

Linfeng finally called her back home after what sounded like a
long day

a waitress swept up the leaves.

Mayor Ma had apparently called Linfeng warning

a cruel draft came through the revolving doors

her head was on the block.

Although there was tension after Meizhu mentioned Old Yu's
arrest in the lobby

a vast tank of live fish she would help.

After all Linfeng had profited from Meizhu's businesses over the
years

fish mouths pressed against the glass. Linfeng's eldest was
studying overseas gasping hopelessly

the expenses endless.

We'll see what we can do, sister.

Meanwhile Linfeng said that she had bad news to share
unfortunately

a young chef in whites approached the tank with a net.

Meizhu's brother Pang Jianhua hadn't been answering his phone all
day

the chef stood on a chair to dip his net inside.

According to Linfeng's information many drivers had taken
strikers to the square without asking for fares

the chef netted a flapping carp.

Meizhu realized that her no good rotten lover Fat Pang was
probably causing trouble for her in the night

fish thrashed about.

I'll find him, big sister.

The Strike

Meizhu cursed reckless Fat Pang as she went back inside she didn't care who whispered about her lifestyle. She'd made it further in life than most in their frozen town her two divorces were notorious.

Hey baby, I was getting lonely.

He was Dong Hongqi as Meizhu approached moodily his cigarette dropped ash on the table. He and Meizhu had first met during her southern buying trip last summer the garlic prawns soaking his fingers in a white silk dress. Unable to forget that one night of steamy passion on the banks of the west lake the debris of their feast was everywhere.

As he messily stubbed out his cigarette on a bed of pink shells Meizhu glowered. They left the restaurant still talking business in fox furs and leather boots she repelled his advances.

Why don't we nail this over a drink?

She was Pan Meizhu felt irritated with this small merchant's crude insinuation despite the thick darkness clouds faintly visible. She had to find her boyfriend in this deepening storm as she walked away Hongqi cackled:

You know you want my big cock!

Meizhu marched across the top of empty Zhongyou Square formless ghosts flitted in the street lamps. She thought soulfully about how she had started her rise fifteen years ago most of these department stores cages of steel. She'd moved back in with her ma and pa for a few months after the failure of her first marriage her father froze into angry silence. To escape his disapproval she locked herself in the bathroom day after day the window displays of the exotic Zhongyou Mall taunted them with a bright new era.

You were young, so damn young.

Her first husband was the pampered only son of a big Suifen cadre for a few months they'd been fairly happy. The traffic lights took ages as the softie drifted home from his secure state job at the same time each day she'd come to realise the road was empty of cars. Times were changing with the reforms he couldn't adapt after less than one year she wanted out. Before finally leaving she'd thought a lot about who the winners might be in their get rich first era the moon smothered by clouds.

You shocked everyone.

Her father felt their family had lost face and started an epic sulk that lasted for years she wanted to kill herself.

One Summer an old classmate who managed a state hosiery factory told her he had a warehouse stuffed full of unsold socks her mother wept herself to sleep. She took a few boxes to sell in their town's first private market just south of Zhongyou Square smoke from a kebab stand made her eyes water.

She sensed restlessness permeating the universe in her bones mysterious dark matter. On a whim she ducked into the once familiar market along Changping Road new year bunting strung from lamposts.

For the first time in ages she saw Old Hu her ally from those market days his wispy beard inside his dog fur coat a snowflake flurry. She smiled fondly at the start kind Old Hu was virtually the only trader to accept her. He always stood up for her as an outsider this cold night there were few customers.

Hi Little Pan, be careful, something's going down tonight.

She'd worked the pitch opposite Hu's butcher's slab for three years lamb hearts bleeding on sheets of newspaper. Most people had closed minds at that time her family looked down on people working for themselves. Because she gave them a share of her earnings after one month her parents' home took delivery of their first microwave oven.

Oh you were brave, really damn brave.

She left Old Hu and hurried on through the cold winds seemed to howl from the past. She had been lucky to enjoy success quickly back then everyone wanted imported goods not for sale inside deer skin boots numb toes.

During her second summer at the market she'd met this hot young taxi driver greasy long hair shooting pool. Strangely she seldom thought about their relationship these days as if he'd never existed they had a kid together.

You were reckless, so reckless.

He was darkly handsome their first time on the worn green felt of the pool table taking him as a fellow rebel cue expertly maneuvered. He often invited her to eat with other drivers the food street's shifting constellation of soy-splattered surfaces. Her parents of course thought this man beneath her he looked comfortable in his skin trying to bring her pleasure.

What a loser.

She turned left onto Yanan Road ten years ago they rented her first boutique here. After their daughter came along year after year she worked hard to sell fashion from down south new ways gradually spread. As a female entrepreneur she became a symbol of their town's development after a few years trading up to a bigger shop. When business really took off she asked her husband to sell his taxi although the roads were empty the traffic lights took ages.

You worked alright, damn hard, for all you've got.

She supposed she became a small celebrity locally because of her success as a woman her husband leaked confidence. He still drove his taxi from dawn to dusk, their shy daughter mostly lived with her parents. Quite often he disappeared all night playing pool bitterly she slipped and almost fell. Regrets were pointless as danger haunted the night the pavements tilted under her heels.

Life never damn stands still.

Around five years ago everyone started playing the market in their city nothing holding steady. The new elite hunched over their screens in smoky stock shops that sprang up around town the skyline a mirage. Society was transformed by new wealth from the border trade day after day she went there to study. Back then everyone thought the market could only go in one direction she hobbled along on her sore feet.

While learning what she could in the stock shop she met Fat Pang for the first time a glimmer of hope. She couldn't help but be impressed by a local man who dressed well in the shadows across the road a stranger watching her. One stock shop manager confided that Mr Pang was married to a mayor's daughter and had invested one million in only a few weeks her pace quickened. For the first time since the early days with her second husband here was someone who attacked life full tilt she reached the corner.

You couldn't bloody help yourself.

Yanan Road felt haunted tonight she drifted through empty space. Slowly she approached People's Square in the unquiet dark voices made her uneasy. Small lights burned around the site of the demonstration as she advanced across a winter gutted footbridge sirens howled.

One day Fat Pang told her with lewd directness he'd booked a hotel room since the footbridge was icy the moon peeping out. She'd always been faithful to her second husband despite opportunities to stray in the Far East Hotel the sheets slid superbly soft. Their appetites turned out to be similar she smiled thinking of Fat Pang's lechery ice melting where hot water leaked from a pipe. He even used their real names when they checked into the hotel later the pipes would soon freeze again.

We're all prisoners of society.

Both families blamed her after Fat Pang's wife found out the bridge was dangerously slippery. They were jealous and called her a whore coldly she gripped the railing for support. Any of them could have succeeded like her she thought she might slip silently into the frozen dark below.

Screw those bastards.

She agreed at last to what her husband asked the wind moaned around the bridge. Although many said it was natural for a man like Fat Pang to stray at family parties she was frozen out and the tangled reeds on the bank looked prehistoric.

After that she couldn't feel pity for the army of ghosts that would never work again after the workshops went dark this city quiet as a graveyard. They'd kept their distance ever since her first divorce people staying indoors. Why should she feel sympathy their lives gone nowhere cars abandoned oddly on the road.

She was frightened at her fury while icicled factories rusted along Hebin Road how slowly things changed. Down south she saw skies of gleaming new towers but worst of all her live in lover Fat Pang was a total disaster.

There'd been another great scandal after Fat Pang's divorce Meizhu refusing to marry him when he moved in the few cars on the road all government plates. Suspicious of his selfish charm even when pregnant with his daughter the lights of buildings around the square ghostly.

Sure enough as she'd already feared Fat Pang turned out to be a waster living off his family for years Suifen waiting to explode. That million he'd invested actually belonged to his sister so smart and tough the kiosks along Haibin Road were boarded up.

A new elite had transformed their town with fortunes made from border trade the strike's threat spreading. Her sister-in-law Linfeng chief of police was among the clever at ease in the rising current casualties were certain. Linfeng had once buried the charge of Boss Cui's son for manslaughter the Bright Moon plant likely to be sold. At least clever Linfeng understood reality whereas the old factories were caught in their own rust.

All the same Meizhu hearing accusing voices in the mist had to admit she herself hadn't been such a genius in love the cold wind lashed her face.

You've made mistakes, too many mistakes.

Supporting others appeared to be her fate cheeks burning not only their five year old son to care for but Meizhu's teenager by her second husband. Since Fat Pang's own daughter by his ex-wife stayed over at weekends the fridge in their apartment was usually empty.

Their messy family survived through Meizhu's hard work the moon briefly appearing again. Her life was a balancing act which bloody Fat Pang now threatened helping the strikers she heard hurried footsteps. Many enemies would love to cut them down with Fat Pang providing opportunity a lone pedestrian rushed past her.

When she thought about the scandal her lover might bring on them tonight the skies above the square were deeply dark. After months idling around the house against her protests that old fool had gone out and bought a taxi to humiliate her it didn't look like it would snow any more. Because her ex was a taxi driver it was awkward nights Fat Pang just cruised around town taking girls for rides.

He wasn't clever enough to hide it a lot of the time people fished from this bridge. Her spies sent reports of his adventures even in winter you could sometimes buy frozen white fish here. Her contempt for him grew after all she'd been through a grimy tree was scorched by lamplight.

So a year ago she'd spent the night with a handsome sales manager on one of her sourcing trips down south the climate was better. Last summer there was that business with Dong in the West Lake Hotel moonlight sliced into thick ice around the bridge.

This was a long delayed collision between past and future she finally left the bridge and skirted the square. Only one winner would emerge beyond a police line one hundred shadows lighting small fires. As she quickened her search for Fat Pang in these harsh winds from beyond the border stinging faces sensed the inevitable outcome.

There was a mass of police trucks outside City Hall the stars froze above the earth apparently doing nothing. She wasn't fooled by their inaction despite rumours of concessions fortunes at stake. Almost every month she met investors' delegations at mayoral banquets snapping up shares in offices and department stores.

Around the mouth of the square a throng of about twenty taxi drivers waited in the charcoal haze engines cooling to see what would happen. Many drivers had family ties with the Bright Moon plant for generations this town's furnace cooling.

Hi, Sister Pan.

They called out like kids in the fiery dark night of time waiting for action. Some of them were eating fried chicken pieces in paper boxes as she approached music blaring from the cars. Because of her ex she was well known among the taxi men many secretly fancied her. The fried chicken was from that giant new supermarket she smiled at the site of the old timber factory. As it was the biggest in their town people loved to go there from the mayor downwards everything came wrapped in shiny packaging.

Come to join us?

She laughed the laugh that was amour above the jangle of canto pop asking if they'd seen Fat Pang. Although they liked Pang because he |owned his own car this sentimental music grated. They slaved night and day to pay for their taxis in all fairness Fat Pang didn't need the singer with a Hong Kong accent. So they didn't mind telling that Fat Pang was down the road in Yellow Moon nightclub
she accepted a swig of snake from their flask.

They explained about Fat Pang taxiing families from the Bright Moon estate her throat burned pleasantly with the drink.

Apparently no one had tried to stop him
hanging from one car mirror a sacred icon.

You be careful friends.

She couldn't help feeling protective of these working men cop sirens blared nearby. According to her instincts it wasn't safe to be caught up in this mess
their cigarettes smouldered silently.

She walked on afterwards sure enough there was Far Pang's big black taxi parked snow scratched sky outside Yellow Moon. Being a restless fool he had obviously got bored sitting with the other drivers in the cold steam gusted out of the door.

The floor was unswept there was a loud mess of beer and talking waitresses ran about in the air. She wasn't surprised after the look on the drivers' faces to see him with a woman as he had little character indeed two. They were about no more than twenty plastered in make up while wearing coats at the table.

'

The Strike

Their breasts tumbled from their black vests the table scattered with a mess of chicken bones and peanut shells and drink. Despite supposedly giving up months ago he smoked a cigar as her skin prickled from unaccustomed warmth.

He was Pang Jianhua flushed face with an arm around the waist of a pretty hostess Meizhu strangely approached him. Away in the wild night for hours he'd felt freedom perhaps just like her second husband before him their bottle was nearly empty. Although drunk for hours he was happy rather than anything else this was inconvenient. Aware that she was striking with her fur and red hair Meizhu ignored the waiters and went straight to the stuffed squirrel on the wall. Without even looking at the dead faced girls in these circumstances she said

your sister is looking for you.

She insisted Fat Pang should stay out of trouble for Linfeng's sake waiters looked on.

Although she meant to stay calm her voice rose and his plate was filled with the remains of dead animals.

Is it true you've been driving people to the bloody square?

She could hardly be bothered to listen to his explanations as the two girls stared why should creatures suffer for decoration. You see he said hand on a bare thigh under the table

the town was coming together now.

She'd never sympathised with ordinary working people he mumbled drunkenly

perhaps her greatest weakness.

Since the girls didn't even pretend to look embarrassed until Meizhu decided to give up and the floor was a mess. She was so angry with him dropping ash from his cigar she didn't bother to suggest peanut shells everywhere. Although futures at stake as always he was careless of the dangers

her heel skidded through spilled beer.

You call your dear sister if you don't want to listen to me.

Yes Jianhua said after she left pouring more snake wine so strong

The Strike

others died drinking it
that was my damn wife.

She's beautiful but cold they laughed unsympathetically deep winter came through the tiled walls.

She was Meizhu waved at a red taxi passing the end of the street a frozen bird dropped to the ground. Rather than go home she called Dong Hongqi at his hotel the bird must have perished in flight.

He was in the hotel sauna waiting for her the taxi rolled over the body. She was so angry her desire startled her as the taxi advanced murderously along the icy surface of her town.

The Strike

5

She was Mrs Zhang asked a crowd over to celebrate Old Yu's release from jail thanks to her friend Meizhu firecrackers snapping in the yard. As she stuffed dumplings for them almost three years ago to the day they had moved to this new apartment. When their daughter Dongmei was young they lived in a hut by the sports ground flour everywhere.

Her thoughts drifted for comfort back to that warm brick hut lined with cardboard dumplings rolled snug in her hand. She floated in spirit along the small dirt track ran past smoke blackened boxes during summer wild flowers blossoming there. Vividly she saw Dongmei as a child reading on the big red chest before her father died cooking smells filled the room.

Although her sister wasn't back yet from the restaurant after Old Yu's retirement Dongmei used her savings to buy her parents this modern home.

That's when it all went wrong.

How unreal their new home seemed when they moved in that autumn afternoon another string of firecrackers snapped in the yard. On entering she and Old Yu froze as if afraid to disturb the gleaming white surfaces a puff of smoke hanging in the air beyond the window. She asked Old Yu what they could put in all the empty wall units a scrawny cat scampering along a row of bins.

Despite the pleasure of their first inside toilet they were like ghosts haunting a world suddenly grown colder. She realised that the core of their lives would always be their time in that brick hut by the sports

The Strike

ground fighting for survival the cat looked hungry.

Any change?

Her big sister Dou Dou entered skin blotches glowing from the Sichuanese restaurant downstairs an icy draft piercing the room. They spooned boxes of mapo tofu and spicy eggplant into bowls as Meizhu said she would join them later fitful breathing came from the bedroom.

The old man's just lying there.

Old Yu had finally returned last night as they put the bowls in the fridge trees shook wildly. Of course she realized he'd never truly loved her because her eyes were teary the branches bare for months.

It's like he's already dead.

Dou Dou helped her heart racing into a chair all winter the sun seemed to have died. Since childhood her stern kind sister had calmed her during edgy moments the wind rattling their windows.

At least he's back now.

Both of them had been reluctant to ask Meizhu for help yesterday a plant pot blew over noisily on the balcony. They became desperate though after no word for ten hours a fire engine wailed past. When Old Yu finally called Dou Dou passed her the phone somewhere in the area of People's Square smoke coils rising.

I'm coming home.

Old Yu's voice sounded normal but she hoped there wasn't fighting in the square.

I'm fine.

Old Yu explained about borrowing the driver's cellphone to call her on his way home in a cop car smoke kept rising denser than death.

Two young cops half carried half dragged him up the stairwell because lights were broken strings of garlic bulbs hung on each landing. When the three of them appeared at their door new year couplets still pasted either side her face couldn't hide her tension.

She froze as they brought Old Yu inside her sister removing his boots. The two lads said we're done with him in the starless night

The Strike

if he keeps out of trouble
doors slamming below.
What are you two staring at?
Old Yu just sat on the sofa with a haunted face she turned up the television. All the while mumbling so as to create an air of normality she fussed with his disheveled hair.
Old Yu, how did you get mixed up in this strike at Bright Moon?
She couldn't understand it when she saw his suffering this night without end. It was as if he'd deliberately got arrested to escape her pulling on a nightgown. She'd cared for him all these years despite everything the nightgown had no belt. Somehow she feared that with Dongmei gone now in their shiny new apartment he would just disappear.
Take Old Yu his medicine.
One cup of sour black liquid in her hand she opened the bedroom door to bring Old Yu his medicine their guests arriving soon. Old Yu lay stiff as a brush in their shared bed piled with clothes hardly acknowledging her.
You still alive? You look terrible.
She wasn't sure because of an old calendar on the wall whether he was alive for a horrible moment.
Have you even slept?
He was Old Yu noticing his wife's curly black hair he didn't feel like answering questions. Although people were protesting in the frosty air south of the border he didn't deserve to be saved. When she held her hand before his mouth to prove that he was breathing stubbornly he turned away.
What's wrong dear?
Yesterday at the police station so many forms his mind spun with frequent crossings out. Officer Zhang made such a big deal of every little thing he said in this life nobodies like him hardly got attention.
He didn't understand most of the questions Zhang asked him over the course of an afternoon the station swarmed with coming and

going. Perhaps silence was the best way to avoid incriminating friends Officer Wen took writing duties. For all that their stern voices demanded attention he thought constantly about what happened years ago with his first girlfriend Guihua.

After the questions they locked him up for hours he shivered alone with a tea cup and a toilet bucket. His cell appeared to be a former air raid shelter day sliding to night he lay on the hard low bench. He could think of no one to call on for help in this crisis the bench cold as his bony arse.

Secretly he felt he deserved his arrest clutching a tin mug with a few dry tea leaves. He was glad to be here because of his guilt about Guihua small cockroaches crawling the walls.

Such was his remorse in years gone by he'd have this apprehension of seeing Guihua appear around a corner guards passing his window. He was always haunted by his last sight of her being beaten in the factory yard angry jeers filling his mind.

Poisonous weed.

The army faction made her stand on a small old workbench head bowed the night choked by clouds. Although she looked so slight gleefully every team sent people forward to abuse and punch her the moon fleetingly emerged. One army leader read out the accusation he'd written so abjectly along the lines provided moon cutting through the clouds.

In the middle of the night two cops appearing unexpectedly he was free to go. They implied some mistake after what he'd done the dark felt very deep. On the way home in the van he asked for their phone to call his wife the van's engine kept farting spluttering.

You drink that medicine now dear.

Although his wife asked him about his arrest he hardly listened to her so as to be thirty years ago with Guihua.

Where are you?

Something wasn't right inside him since his arrest medicine trickling down as his wife moved around the room. Beneath the warm blankets he was light years away visiting Guihua for the first time in a hospital bed one late summer afternoon.

You seem lost to me.

Back then three decades ago after a short spell in the army he was an assembly line worker who rarely clocked on at the number three machine factory. There were frequent stoppages because of the political turmoil loudspeakers blared slogans years before his marriage.

His team leader said this young girl Guihua was back from the countryside with shot nerves they'd met before as children. This student had no family sadly he raised his hand and volunteered to visit which was out of character they thought for him. He discovered this frail figure alone in the ward shy eyes under a dark bob of hair smuggling in sweet bread that first time. Although she fainted regularly over several afternoons they shared their stories.

During their early conversations she recounted those months in the countryside learning from farmers her feet blistered and split. She described thirty city girls on rations in one stinky hut naturally comrades got on each other's nerves. Her eyes still shone with idealism as he had little appetite eating most of the sweetmeats. Such contradictions were common enough in students he found they only fuelled his attraction for her. Despite the dangers the two of them grew intimate in the metal-boned bed Guihua's sticklike body warm and vulnerable.

He had his tales too after schools were closed fifty classmates had walked for a week to join the events in the national capital their feet aching. They pressed shoulder to shoulder at rallies for a glimpse of senior leaders he remembered most clearly there were no toilets. Nights in makeshift dormitories boys and girls sharing mattresses under cover of dark he confessed a lot secretly going on. That was the excuse he sighed deeply for warmth failing to believe anything in particular.

One morning their dorm captain sent them to a courtyard

somewhere near the palace museum a traitor being denounced. The old general bowed his white head to sate revolutionary fury they smashed precious heirlooms to the ground. Although he didn't feel right about hurting this grandfather a blue vase broke thrillingly into a thousand pieces.

After two months Guihua left hospital and started work at his factory production collapsing. The place was messed up by warring factions bringing work to a near standstill he tried to keep his head down.

There was fighting all over town under the protection of central authorities their plant supposedly did vital work for the nation. At the most tense times stray flying bullets he slept over with Guihua and her roommate.

People still had to venture out for food despite the corpses in the street he took care of them. Guihua trusted him like a sister when they were alone inside her red nightdress nattering for hours. The factory often closed daytimes taking quiet walks by the river you never knew when someone might take a shot at you.

The excitement began to make everyone half crazy troops rumoured to be arriving from down south. Some weeks there were surging marches in the streets before they collapsed into chaos he
even went with her a few times. He had this feeling his universe expanded with Guihua more than once they saw traitors' bodies floating beneath Suifen Bridge.

While the fighting peaked Guihua and her faction of red sister rebels demanded rebellion at the factory a red hot summer. They blitzed the grounds with posters denouncing their boss as a counterrevolutionary the noon sun unbearably fierce. No air conditioning back then heat rising he felt secretly pleased when she asked him to write words for the posters.

She praised his characters the bristling brush writing her slogans time and space unravelled.

So why had he betrayed her days later the army arrived to support the rival faction and restore order. He'd beat up himself thinking about that over the years his wife touching his head.

You must get up and meet our guests.

His head dizzy even now the magnitude of his mistake seeming undiminished. Yesterday his banner waving above People's Square he'd seen Guihua's ghost denouncing him bitterly his legs flexed.

Get up now and see your nephew.

She wasn't dead but had married a deer farmer in the windswept five colour valleys his wife rubbed his arm. The man passed away though he'd heard last year her hands felt soft. He let his wife help him from the bed outwards as if in a dream it didn't seem like his life at all.

Where are your slippers, the comfortable ones?

His wife guided Old Yu's feet down to the floor as a husband never being fully there for her. He sought his slippers throughout their married life Guihua living just ten miles away. Hs nephew's throaty laugh came from the kitchen Guihua seeming more real than any of them.

What the hell trouble have you been in, Uncle?

Although Old Yu's face turned purple whenever he drank loud nephew Lin Mu waved a bottle of Suifen beer in his direction.

Uncle is free, let's celebrate!

Lin Mu was a gregarious sales rep for the Bright Moon plant marrying an asthmatic accountant. Ten years ago he failed his college entrance exam by a few marks to his mother's relief everyone appreciated his good temperament. The plant often asked him to entertain customers on this account showing them a beam of stained teeth.

Lin Mu was close with Old Yu's girl Dongmei in the old days their glasses filled to the brim. When Old Yu remembered that Dongmei had been gone for years now against doctor's orders he took a great gulp.

Old Yu can really drink.

The Strike

Lin Mu tactfully ignored Old Yu's misfortune telling about his attempt to hire a cheap Santana for a family wedding the bowls warmed again. He made them laugh recounting his conversation with the hire company dumpling steam perfumed the room.

I want my coffin made from wood, not metal!

From habit Dou Dou frowned at her son's idle chatter although she loved him a few dumplings were overfilled. One bad score in Lin Mu's math test had spoiled his chances of college raising a bulging dumpling to her mouth the pork mince slid out. Secretly she'd been jealous when Dongmei did well in her high school exams the others cackling.

You're something else, Lin Mu.

They started to eat although Meizhu hadn't arrived last year's calendar was still nailed to the wall. The conversation got round to the Bright Moon protests since Lin Mu's wife worked there the calendar had images of migrating birds.

It's been coming a damn long time.

With his usual fluency Lin Mu told them about the strike while praising the overseasoned pork dumplings. Since the government made money from shuttering the timber works until the Bright Moon sale was the last straw for most people

he drained his glass.

What the hell's really going on in People's Square?

Lin Mu admitted he'd only been in the square for a few minutes he liked the shrimp ones too.

For his family's sake it was better not to get too involved although he sympathized with the protestors the shrimp were particularly bloody good.

We're not all as brave as you, Old Yu.

Seeing Old Yu's emotional look Lin Mu added quickly he'd heard there were hundreds refusing to leave People's Square

echoing faintly through the kitchen steam.

That jerk Mayor Ma came out apparently

detained sirens still in the air.

The mayor?

Yeah Lin Mu said the mayor invited the union leaders to enter City Hall but the whole crowd surged uncontrollably

nothing to be done.

Greetings, friends.

Pan Meizhu arrived late from the deep night snow on her wool hat. She wore a dead fox pelt across her shoulders that lovelorn dog of hers Pang Jianhua trailing. Mrs Zhang quickly served more dumplings from the still steaming pot tension suffused the room.

Have something Mrs Zhang said aware that many people didn't like Meizhu

out came spicy eggplant from the downstairs restaurant.

Thank you, we won't stay long.

Meizhu sat down behind Old Yu a picture of a wild swan spreading its broad wings with a meaningful look maintaining

they would dine later.

We're on our way to a reception.

Pang Jianhua launching himself at the awkward silence that followed with brimming glass as usual Meizhu felt fed up. The others laughed loyally as Fat Pang toasted Old Yu in that phony way she faced a wall of unfriendly eyes. They only stopped by Mrs Zhang's place to be polite on the way she'd never realised these deadbeat relatives were invited too.

So you've been a bad boy, Old Yu?

She was Meizhu seething mad inside ever since catching Fat Pang with those young girls he kept bragging about helping the strikers. They had seemed to hang on his every word that same night

taking her revenge at Dong Hongqi's hotel.

We taxi drivers were shoulder to shoulder with the Bright Moon workers.

He exaggerated his role so much the smell of the shrimp dumplings almost making her retch. Once she found him charming but these days the thought of eating sea life strangely repulsed her.

Later there was a reception at the Zhongyou Department Store
despite the strike pushing away her plate.

When they saw how many we were they folded and just let us
drive through.

What Meizhu didn't know was in one of his past lives Fat Pang
was the privileged son of a courtier. An entitled waster he lived for
jousting and seducing pretty boys in theatres. One of the fathers
complained to the court shortly after Fat Pang was lashed and thrown
out of town.

She scowled because Fat Pang was bragging about his heroism in
the thick of the action filling her glass with beer.

A damn lot you know about it!

Although Meizhu was usually disciplined in public the cold beer
made her shudder. As the others fell silent with increasing fury she
and Fat Pang exchanged insults.

You've never done a day's work in your life.

I've always bloody worked.

You don't understand normal people.

I'm more normal than you.

Finally she yelled

Bright Moon workers are losers

all around the table

hurt faces

clinging to the past.

Why should the government give them any more money forgetting
Mrs Zhang's relatives worked at Bright Moon who owes them
anything.

Don't you see the world has changed she claimed passionately
they hated her.

Why should we change what works?

Lin Mu spoke up with what sounded like bewilderment Meizhu
draining her beer.

The Strike

Our parents and grandparents built this town from nothing Lin Mu claimed

over many years making sacrifices.

We generated power for half the north east in the past

Bright Moon counted for something.

You can't forget the past Jiahui's dumb looking sister echoed dumplings going cold.

The past counts for something Old Yu agreed apparently miles away.

The past continues Lin Mu said

as Meizhu listened

truly unreal.

These ghosts had let themselves become nothing the night continuing outside. They might have deserved pity except that they'd been hostile all her life pushing back her chair.

Everyone looked at their feet shadows lengthening. It was pointless to stay now they were late for the city reception up she got.

Mrs Zhang saw them to the door awkwardly others trying to make conversation.

How is young Dongmei getting on?

At the mention of his daughter Old Yu stared blankly beyond the window space flooded with darkness Meizhu leaving. Strikes were matters for the living ever since what befell Guihua all those years ago he felt like the living dead.

The Strike

6

He was Chen Yun waking that next morning the world still sunk in darkness the floor aunty brought a hot water flask to his room. She smiled shyly light entering from the corridor he saw that she wasn't the type to listen at doors.

Afterwards he drew the curtains cheerfully shop workers with white coats and brooms brushing dirty ice off the road. This task seemed better organised than in his home town even the slagheaps were snow-glazed. His darkness had lifted after last night's despair a donkey cart trotted down the main street.

He wasn't sure this feeling would last as today's sun came up few others did. He was a survivor at least splashing cold water on his face which they couldn't take away from him. He was almost over his wife having walked out six months ago starting to shave. He wouldn't think about his daughter now razor gliding around his neck there were other matters.

He felt a sense of optimism associated with that young miss last night shower taps running. She came to him from nowhere at what felt like his darkest hour testing the temperature. She held him like a lover for ten minutes or so before requesting payment the water came in fits and starts. They would meet today hopefully he stood under the shower.

Increasingly starving he left for breakfast before noon the was sun an orange squib in a charcoal sky. Stopping at a basement breakfast shop he ordered a bowl of spicy noodles in a brown sauce mouth watering. As he ate the noodles with an egg floating on top he thought carefully what to say to the young miss about his contact at Bright Moon. The waiter brought him a beer remembering her warm ffragrance he told himself not to imagine too much.

Although it wasn't noon he almost ran back to the hotel to call her snow underfoot streets were slippery. As they talked a vacuum cleaner whining in the next room she seemed hardly to remember him. Her voice sounded so distant Chen Yun even wondered whether or not this was her the vacuum cleaner banged violently against the dividing wall. He was going to hang up as the banging drove him crazy, until unexpectedly she agreed to meet him.

On his way there the world drifting as if in a dream this city's slender birches contrasted with his home town's banyans. He had never seen such straight proud trees in the scratched ice street lay a sick skinny dog. Stopping for a smoke outside the old theatre by the station the hound growled hungrily strangers walked by.

Happy Future Mall seemed like a prosperous fort at the end of history his pockets empty. Outside the front door he bought a red rose wrapped in newspaper the split toe of his left boot gaping.

Police were stopping cars at a junction back home his wife and daughter might be answering questions. Because of them he almost turned back until the pouting sign of the Pink Lipstick café appeared ahead the snow swept into heaps.

You came, Little Xu.

His night visitor finding him in a corner after she came in the idle waiter turned on the music. The less she said the more it touched him when a wisp of long hair escaped from her furry hood.

What's this for?

She looked painfully thin inside her padded black jacket taking his red rose cautiously Chen Yun supposed she was recently arrived from some very poor village.

Don't you like it he said after giving her a few notes as well she nodded and stuffed them inside her black jacket

he wanted nothing.

The Strike

How long have you been in this dog city?

She murmured for months

Chen Yun would remember the fragrance of her skin.

Chatting in a soft voice she asked him to call her little sister occasionally the waiter stared at them. He wanted to earn her trust the waiter delivering fruit salad with a scoop of coconut sorbet.

I got up late today.

Little Xu looked thin as she chased fruit pieces around her bowl he brought their conversation back to Bright Moon.

You said your Uncle might meet me.

He reminded Little Xu about his friend a cockroach scuttling under the table. The young woman seemed to have forgotten everything from last night the creature another intruder.

You really want to see him?

Little Xu ate her dessert hungrily he watched the door certain that someone would come for him.

That's up to you.

He wondered what her life had been like since leaving her village the sorbet already gone.

Uncle's family doesn't have many visitors.

After finishing her sweet Little Xu used a cellphone bound with elastic bands to make a call balloons hung from the ceiling. Someone asked her a lot of questions above their heads one white balloon burst like a gunshot.

After hanging up, she checked her lipstick in the metal wall panel tarnished shadow for a moment their future uncertain.

Shall we get the hell out of here?

On such a cold day after leaving the restaurant he felt everyone noticed them since Huahe Road was sealed off following her east to a block of untidy small shops with a taxi rank.

So what do you do then?

After they had their car he sat with her explaining about his job back home

she gave directions.

The Strike

Her scent of shampoo and skin was strong in the car's heat they just missed the lights.

You work for the government?

Not government but a union as they passed the Northern Bank she put her hand on his leg.

What's the difference?

She was Xu Yue supposing the guy had money being a cadre they were close to the old timber works. He was more interesting than many clients in her eyes the new supermarket glittered with things she couldn't afford.

So you get an apartment and everything?

Yeah he said the young woman's hand resting still between his legs an ordinary two room unit.

Chen Yun described the apartment because of the dry winter his lips cracked with dryness.

Xu Yue tried to imagine the modern kitchen bedrooms on a high floor the taxi thick with warmth.

Do you travel much?

She saw him as a man of the world the driver kept the blower on full.

Sometimes Chen Yun told her a few years ago the sky stretched cold and pale he spent a fortnight in the capital. Staying in some newly built hotel downtown unable to sleep because of traffic he longed for the refreshing cold outside. Driving towards her uncle's house Chen Yun mentioned a park where he'd half jogged half walked around a lake every morning

Xu Yue liking the smoky roughness of his voice.

Where's your wife?

He was Chen Yun thought what his wife would say if she could see him cruising with this youngster inside his clothes back sweaty. The suburbs became more like villages of muddy huts increasingly he found it hard to remember his wife's face.

Don't have one. Maybe you'll marry me.

She was Xu Yue smiling with her hand still on her client's knee the car turned into a lane. Once a boy had proposed to her on the way home from school although people said he was a bit simple one bump jolted her skywards. This kid died in an accident years ago the pockmarked lane was rough. As they passed between rows of muddy huts she laughed to show she hadn't taken her client's words seriously a three legged dog limping alongside the car.

Your uncle lives here?

The taxi couldn't go further on the rough track they paid the driver walking the rest of the way. This lane was where Xu Yue lived with her aunt and uncle after first arriving in the city the lame dog still followed them. Her night job in the Happiness Bar was an embarrassment for her aunt the dog looked hungry. Actually she really hated to come back here because people called her names the dog found a pile of chicken bones.

Uncle's house stood made of long and thick red bricks chickens in a cage in the yard.

You're here.

Xu Yue's younger cousin Jiabao was brewing tea in the green- tiled kitchen on seeing them sunlight broke through the window. This was the first time Yue had brought a man home during the day Jiabao's knuckles looked red from the hot water. The sun sparkled on soap bubbles in the sink because such different characters they somehow got on.

You know the way, sister.

Entering a living room stuffed with heavy furniture the two guests were asked to sit. After an eternity Xu Yue's uncle appeared brandishing a bottle on the boxy television gymnasts.

It's cold outside.

Because Xu Yue trusted her uncle she explained about Chen Yun as one gymnast in a red leotard tried a triple somersault. Uncle Xu listened while pouring shots of snake the young gymnast's grace might well win her the competition.

As Chen Yun launched into his story Aunty Lin entered the room with touching modesty the competitor beaming shyly. I need to find a union boss at Bright Moon, Zhou Anguo.

The judges held up scorecards nine and ten silently sturdy Aunty Lin sat on a chair arm peeling an apple.

Uncle Xu's ears tufted with gray hair explaining Anguo's reputation the table gleamed with spilled snake wine.

He stood and refilled their glasses just yesterday
he'd been with Old Zhou's son.
You won't have bloody heard.

His eyes sparkled as he told them about the strike at Bright Moon both bars of the electric heater blazing angrily.

It's a moment of history.

You see he said first those bastards shuttered the timber works lighting a cigarette
before selling the bloody bus station. After that they forced unpaid
overtime at the
rubber plant
hundreds laid off.

When the rotten dogs said Bright Moon was next lying we were
broke before we knew it
everything exploding.
The town fought back!

He was Xu Dongfang couldn't really describe being in People's Square that day so many comrades voicing feelings they'd not imagined the doors of City Hall ever opening. That sense of rebellion had stayed with him since new year the weather dial stuck on bleak.

Over the years he explained their city became divided like a bad dream
the snake wine in his glass kept vanishing.

Life long party folk were burning their own membership cards he laughed from personal experience
there was another bottle behind the television.
Ask my wife.

The Strike

Aunty Lin told them in her throaty voice she'd joined the party on her tenth birthday

a parade for the revolution's anniversary. Government cars rode in front as children proceeded with red armbands and banners

their next door neighbour arrested recently.

Her face clouded over suspiciously trees rattled outside the window.

You're Mr Zhou's friend?

He was Chen Yun seeing Little Xu's uncle and aunt as like his comrades from the pit fires blazing outside the gates. He'd fought alongside his people for months to achieve justice magpies on the trees abruptly alighted.

The old world is falling apart.

He described waves of strikes washing across their province all year wages unpaid the others listening cautiously. With a national congress scheduled soon he said his boss Old Wang got the idea of everyone heading south

the snake wine's aftertaste of woodshavings.

A march?

Down south?

You know said Uncle Xu all of a sudden Chen Yun talking too wildly

we heard Anguo was in hospital.

Yes said Aunty Lin slowly remembering

Chen Yun was a stranger after all

the curtains were never fully closed.

You say you've never actually met Old Zhou?

Chen Yun realised he'd talked too passionately a clock ticking. He'd forgotten the need for caution when Uncle and Aunty's generation were young they suffered from history.

I don't want any trouble.

Where's Mr Chen staying Aunty asked Little Xu pointedly before he could warn her a car revved in the lane outside.

As Xu Yue said the name of his hotel a dog barked in the hallway her young cousin hanging on her every word.

Hey sister, is that the hotel where you work?

She was Jiabao admired her cousin from the bottom of her heart the three legged mutt had somehow followed them inside Xu Yue seemed nervous. She hoped her father wouldn't drink all night again whatever everyone thought one day she would have a boyfriend.

Only when I feel like it.

Xu Yue was desperate to get the hell out hating their questions the three legged dog jumped around Jiabao in a green dress clinging to her. She hadn't visited Aunty and Uncle for weeks now she remembered why it was already dark no stars above.

We'll let Old Zhou's family know about you.

They all went out in the lane Uncle said we wish you would move back with us again all knowing that wasn't true on this dim winter afternoon

waiting together for a taxi.

The longer they stood there the more Chen Yun could feel Aunty Lin's suspicion hanging in the lane with no street lights.

You will go back to the hotel?

Although the dog still barked waiting for transport Xu Yue didn't want Chen Yun now. When the three wheeler arrived covered with a plastic wind shield she snapped she had to get ready for Yu Wen later. As they sped back towards town her client said do what you like their bodies shaking on the bony metal seat.

I'm tired.

When Chen Yun offered to take Little Xu home she refused at first the dog running alongside the taxi. After she relented and leaned against him for a moment he thought maybe she did have feelings for him after all the sun returning tomorrow. Her right hand pressed between his bony knees there might be snow any minute. Little Xu's lips mouthing song lyrics in the rushing air she looked like a pop star.

The Strike

You should give me more money.

His fingers caressed the line of her thin hair above the high collar of her black jacket doubts returned. Although beautiful he wondered why he was chasing after her the moon appeared in brief glimpses. What might happen like last time he gave her one hundred.

No doubt he'd made a mess of things with loose talk in front of Little Xu's family a line of migrating birds not looking back. Although they seemed like decent people when you thought about it her life was already hard. He had no one to rely on as the cab wove deeper inside a thicket of tall scabrous apartment blocks the air thickening around them.

I will sleep.

After Little Xu got out looking through the window with an air of uncertain invitation a bird spread its wings above the courtyard.

Goodbye Little Xu.

All the while she walked away Chen Yun's eyes followed her through the gate. Somewhere above in the late afternoon a single red light glowed in a window which floor he couldn't tell. Amid the empty panes it felt like hers telling the driver his hotel he had a strange feeling about that blood red window

The Strike

7

When the strike began suddenly lost in dawn twilight he was Zhou Junjie the union chief's son. Because his father was under police guard in hospital morning uncertain comrades turned to him. After heavy snowfall they marched along the road of the Bright Moon estate as the gale howled past the middle school and foreign experts guesthouse.

Eventually they reached People's Square oddly enough snow still fell on dozens of government workers sweeping the road outside City Hall. More comrades came through the streets of their town taxi drivers offering free rides. With his father absent Junjie was the symbol of leadership now above the square the skies brightening. Although he wasn't senior as a chill wind blew the father's authority passed to the son.

His colleagues demanded action while local restaurants supplied free rice boxes steaming with fury and determination he'd never felt involved in anything this huge. The crowds grew and grew by mid morning a hill of rice boxes and water bottles rose above them banners waiting for words. Running along the embankment to recruit Old Yu as a weak ray of sunlight broke through the mist he felt history gathered in him.

After dark Mrs Gao and the other union cadres took him to the hospital because his father's leadership was so important soldiers had sealed the ward. They withdrew for hours of debate at the Boiling Point Hotpot Restaurant thin slices of bacon bubbling in the broth. Some thought they should end it before arrests began polishing off a bottle of snake wine others said order more. Mrs Gao loyally insisted nothing could be decided without his father debate raged until the second bottle drained

leaving the night behind.

He reached home after midnight. Jiaying was apparently asleep although he was exhausted the lights off in the kitchen. Jiaying had left a note saying Old Yu was arrested that afternoon slumping down on a chair.

What could you do when your damn wife loathed you no more cigarettes. What could you do when she turned her back on you with trembling hands lighting the last one.

Were the hell could they go to escape this kitchen light flickering flickering and buzzing.

He went to join his wife dead to the world their huge bed filled two thirds of the room.

He stripped off his clothes dropped to the floor and crawled under their heavy grey-striped quilt her body curled like a question.

Secretly he longed for her loving touch was she dreaming outside the world so dark. He thought she was asleep but she let slip a fart apparently something was wrong with their relationship. Her soft emission disturbed the still of the room by the dresser there were misshapen shadows. Heart beating loudly beneath a cotton sleepdress he couldn't work her out at all. Was it possible his mind was too tired for a sleeping person to fart. She might be pretending at night the heating was turned up a long way.

While their universe unraveled in the dimness he found himself worried not about the strike running hot outside but her cold heart barely visible. When they first met eight years ago Jiaying was a new graduate with a compact body from the technical college. Although she was more educated than him they had turned out to be compatible in unforeseen ways their son arrived.

For months now they'd been at war as their love stretched thinner than ever resenting his involvement with the union. Some weeks he hardly saw her except to eat his brain wouldn't turn off. She was denying him comfort at this critical time shadows stretched across the ceiling.

At first light freezing in the courtyard before she even woke he went straight back to the square. A low band of clouds set in from mid morning Mrs Gao and the other union leaders were on the defensive because a rumour spread his father was in secret talks with the plant bosses.

Since yesterday most of the Bright Moon comrades had been including Junjie until today the sun hadn't really come up and his lungs felt dry.

Over and again this morning chants shook the air unexpectedly the hated Mayor Ma emerged sweating on the steps of City Hall. He appeared to invite their leaders for discussion a brace of magpies flew over and shat on his head. The rowdy crowd surged towards the doors of City Hall with bawdy jeers the birds scattered.

No comrades, not all of us.

No one wanted to miss out at this historic moment voices rung like gun shots in the frozen square Mrs Gao shrieking to hold back.

Your appointed leaders will represent you, comrades.

Anger grew shouting shoving and pushing the doors caving in they charged into the building. The fractious crowd was channeled into a municipal conference room paneled with pine at one end of the century.

After Mayor Ma appeared the worse for wear on the platform the crowd howled with contempt. They were the masters now in his wildest fantasies Junjie had never imagined an official treated so disrespectfully.

We won't let you sell us out.

The workers demanded justice until Mayor Ma left the stage feebly sun came through high windows. They waited impatient on this afternoon of anger perhaps time would undo all injustice.

The afternoon sun swept low across the stage the mayor

reemerged with bigshots including Zhou Anguo. At the sight of his father the crowd's roar swelled under the wooden roof life came from stardust.

We're in this together.

As they watched Father stand with the bosses the crowd's angry murmur grew quickly for that sector of the universe. They suspected betrayal as the mayor struggled for attention someone turned and spat on the floor.

Comrades, we've reconsidered our decision.

Fighting for a hearing Mayor Ma said how can we renew our community in this remote place

wind rattling the high windows.

He failed to impose his authority on the meeting full of empty hate ghosts trying to enter.

We don't trust you.

Suddenly his father stepped towards the front of the stage to Junjie's horror taking the loudspeaker in his big hands silence.

Comrades, we have won..

The familiar deep tones boomed within this murmuring chamber his face tired and gray. Although his words filled the pine lined room the skies were beyond with their fate.

No more talk of 'us' and 'them'.

A sense of humiliation welled inside him several voices asked why his father defended the bosses. He sensed anger from all sides in this northern wasteland with no answer to their problems his father pressed a hand to his chest.

Hours later he finally slipped away almost unnoticed night had come in their bed Jiaying browsing a psychology forum. This was an unloving wife so indifferent for weeks because of the pollution there were no stars.

You're ruining our family.

Unexpectedly she spoke to him a few weeks ago cycling home a comet descending. Since she'd held in her emotions all these weeks

The Strike

the comet seeming cold with fury too.

you ignore me/ causing trouble at Bright Moon/ like a wife should do/ neglecting your own family/ while I fight for us/ you're no father/ what kind of woman/everything is fucked/fucked

She was the picture of a smug college girl sat on the nightstand a vase of dead reeds.

Because he would never forgive her entitled air as he had no degree the reeds giving out a faintly rotten smell. Shoving her along the bed harder than he meant for that superior face the vase of reeds rolled off.

Cold.

The vase shattered as the wind moaned sharply he heard Jiaying's head slam on the bedboard. She struck back at him through a curtain gap the moon silently condemned.

Heartless.

As he struggled to pin her flailing wildly a tree rattled in the wind outside. Contorted with fury he seemed to lose his mind scraping against the window with his fingernails determined to claw away that smugness.

You should respect me.

Feeling all his frustration erupt he pushed the back of her legs high into the air an alarm clock went flying. As if hypnotised he stared smudgy dark folds an unfurled red slash where life enters from beyond the curtains unknowable darkness. Although he knew he was doing something very wrong millions of years ago life had emerged from the sea.

Bastard.

With piston hands he rocked her legs as if in a trance upwards and backwards night coiled like a spring. Although he hadn't got drunk tonight she still fought back over millenia a rotating disc of gas and dust formed.

You treat me like I'm nothing.

All his life he supposed he'd remember this night love died until a cry came from the doorway they'd never thought about the noise. Their son cowered behind his father's guilty back the whole rotten universe shrinking to this one room.

Get out. Now.

ii.

Wei Jiaying had fallen out of love through their bedroom window a gloomy row of trees. She sat beside her father in law for days their bathroom pipes frozen.

We've always got on.

She listened to her father in law try and talk her out of leaving on the bed it was true they'd always been close. She even wondered sometimes their legs lightly touched whether she had married Junjie because of liking her manly father in law.

Junjie's been under pressure lately with this strike.

Guilty she remembered how she'd seen father in law naked one summer afternoon her hair felt oily and shit.

Surely you can forgive my son.

She'd returned from the shops late that afternoon flowers still lay where they'd fallen on the floor desperate for a wee. The door wasn't locked after she entered the vase broken in half father in law was in there drying himself. While her heart raced they started at each other in stunned silence the heirloom couldn't be mended.

Aiya.

Wei Jiaying had no way to know that several lifetimes ago she was a maid chosen to serve within a young prince's palace hidden chambers. Her parents hoped she might rise to concubine status because of her good education taking the payment offered. Unfortunately the wealthy prince died early according to custom all eighty-one maids nine concubines and three wives were buried alive with him.

The Strike

A man needs his wife's affection.

With a shy smile she remembered how hairy his body had looked since her own dad died painfully from cancer years ago due to his charm perhaps Father in law was a replacement.

You have been ignoring him.

She hadn't meant her strike to last so long in bed never feeling Junjie's touch. Somehow she just felt smothered at home her mother always visiting. Surely she should never forgive him for how he treated her that night in the bedroom a smell of vase water still lingered.

I hate him.

She had felt sensitive about her body that night spreading her legs like a doctor their son had seen everything. She always thought she was ugly down there in their small life the worst thing was how a divorce would hurt Little Pig.

You two can get past this.

With her repetitive customs job for which she was overqualified where was the carefree life of just a few years ago it seemed they'd been young. Why couldn't her husband find a way to get on in this new world the bathroom pipes frozen for days.

Life's not fair.

Eight years after graduating she leaned on her father in law's broad shoulder several classmates worked for multinationals and sometimes even travelled abroad. Although they had all thought her most likely to succeed she hadn't wanted that enough apparently he rubbed her back. When she saw images of her friends' spacious homes down south she just wanted her husband to do something to excite her. The tension was strangling her father in law claimed doubtfully you know my son loves you.

Junjie should have been retraining and learning skills for the new era she hadn't powdered her face today. How often had she pleaded with him to leave Bright Moon her clothes were all shabby. His loyalty to the union infuriated her while shadows stretched outside the future retreated. His pose of being a leader was especially humiliating because no one respected him the way they did her father in law pulled her closer.

Life seems so damn hopeless.

The years had raced by after accepting a safe job at the customs bureau she married the first person who asked her. For the rest of her life she might pay for that mistake in this town stuck in the past her jeans and shirts were folded on the bed ready to go.

I hate this strike.

Early in their marriage they'd vaguely made plans to leave Suifen and move to a city somewhere down south her tears tasted salty.

What was the point of dreaming now that some man might come and change things like that handsome border trader she thought she would take Little Pig to her parents tonight.

The strike won't last forever.

The border trader usually visited her at the customs bureau when he was in town her old room at her parents' place was still empty. He couldn't come across now she supposed as the border was closed it always felt strange sleeping there again. He represented a timber company on the other side although she was married she found him attractive. The last time she'd actually thought he was about to say something for a moment lying there time froze over.

She felt guilty even thinking about it now all she wanted from her husband was hope she had a cold coming on. She didn't ask for much just small improvements to make life easier her father in law handed her a scented tissue.

After all this is over maybe we can all make a fresh start.

He knew deep down she couldn't hurt her son this year spring seemed later than ever. Although the days were getting longer in the end she let father in law tell her what she had to hear.

You two have a future together.

Confidently he said Young Zhou can find another good job drying her eyes

in a private enterprise. Old horses like me
are only fit for the knacker's yard we envy you
the future.
Not so bad, is it?

iii.

He was union chief Zhou Anguo since the strike broke out this
sickness had got deep into him. That day he addressed comrades at
City Hall he felt very close to death everything falling apart. Mayor
Ma had fetched him personally from the hospital at dawn the smoke
from ten thousand charcoal fires made his chest burn raw.

Since his late wife managed most family issues before passing
from cancer until Jiaying finally smiled so sweetly he stopped
worrying she would leave. However he was still tense because of the
disturbing news just learned from his son they went at once to the
kitchen.

His son at the sink looked round nervously a cold draft entering
through that ancient crack in the window. This time Junjie knew he
had really messed up floating in the dirty water was a stack of spicy
noodle stained pots.

Say you're sorry.

Junjie looked at them with an expression full of childish hurt
drawing her in and embracing her from behind she looked young in
blue jeans. Her arms dangled and splashed aimlessly in soapy water
he didn't think about women so much now he was sick.

You two make up properly now.

Junjie hugged Jiaying with apparent contrition because they
seemed to expect it Anguo made a little speech. Since the strike broke
out he'd been telling people they should unite
in smoky rooms comrades were strongest when standing together.

The Strike

You rest for a while, Pa.

He went next door to give them space to make peace Little Pig sat on his cot repeatedly firing a little ball from a plastic gun.

No homework today?

He lay down on the cot to try and get his thoughts straight Little Pig kept the ball pinging around. He could finally focus on the mysterious stranger who apparently visited his son last night the ball hit the ceiling.

Hey Grandpa, you catch it.

Angry voices came through the wall why should this man according to his son suddenly show up here. His son had said he was a comrade of his friend Old Wang from the Hebin miners' union

the ball ricocheted near to his face.

Are you afraid Grandpa?

Old Wang had appeared in his life about ten years ago he lunged unsuccessfully they were younger then of course. Both were their respective work units' delegates to the annual union conference in the provincial capital he finally managed to get the ball in the cup.

During the conference they got drunk most nights Old Wang paid for hostesses to join them at the Blue Moon Bay KTV club. The hostesses in the provincial capital were attractive especially with snake wine and beer flowing he and Wang bonded.

Afterwards they still talked occasionally there was something charismatic about the man perhaps because of worsening arthritis his hand lacked coordination.

Grandpa, you missed it again.

He remembered a phone call some time around summer's stormy beginning there was flooding of the Suifen River. By then of course he'd already heard rumours about protests in Old Wang's city of Hebin the sewers burst and corrupted the water supply although nothing was officially reported.

While he sympathized with the miners he told Old Wang with practiced bluntness there was no chance of Bright Moon expressing support

last summer one of the stormiest in memory.

Was it likely that Old Wang would send someone here without even a phone call the world supposedly warming up. The authorities strictly forbade coordination between protests in different cities his many enemies were probably trying to frame him.

Grandpa, when can we eat?

He led Little Pig back to the kitchen apparently happier now his daughter in law tight black shirt was frying shredded pork. As the oil made a lot of smoke he realised the threat might come from any side.

What's going to happen about the plant then?

He told his family the arguments had raged until four in the morning the cracked window above the sink would seemingly never be fixed.

But we won. Bright Moon won't be sold for now.

There were a couple of beers in the fridge his son still looked sore about being shut out of the negotiations. They shared a cold one as well as relating a little insider gossip Anguo mollified Junjie with praise for his role in the strike. The beer foamed over after pulling the ring that capitalist roader Boss Cui had been warned his bid for the highway contract would be killed if he made a fuss.

There was a brown froth fountain sure enough Junjie felt important again because his father had confided in him.

This will show those bastards, they can't push us around.

As he listened to his son's bullshit he felt anxious the main kitchen light was flickering. The Bright Moon plant would still be sold in the end humming sickly to a state owned company in another city. This way the Suifen government would profit his eyes ached from the light while keeping the factory in public ownership.

Time will tell.

Although others might swim far in the sea of enterprise his son would drown as Jiaying should well realize the extractor fan was also broken. The fumes made him cough at this moment he didn't have time to worry about his son's lack of spine.

Tell me again about those two coming here.

It seemed Old Xu's niece and the stranger from Hebin had sat right here at this damn table the failing light now whining like a mosquito. His son claimed the pair had seemed harmless as his grandson hid under a chair apparently no one around here had any sense.

He said he knows a friend of yours, father.

Anguo pressed them again for details to make up for lost time his smart daughter in law frying his favourite braised pork noodles. Smoke from spring onions swirled thickly for hours they had waited here. Someone obviously meant to cause him trouble using this stranger he rubbed his stinging eyes. Their once strong family was under attack even before recent events many in the Bright Moon union never trusted him.

This has to be a bloody set up.

Zhou Anguo in one of his previous lives was a captain bravely fighting in the service of his lord thousands slaughtered. One day when the northern general issued a challenge although they tried to stop him because of his age he rode forward from his lines. After seven bouts of exchanges with his opponent being too slow at the turn a deadly arrow skewered the back of his neck.

What are we going to do?

He told them the truth alarmingly the metallic cold beer made his heart race. You were dead wrong to let him in our home he said as the universe full of hidden dark matter

the doctors warned him about his blood pressure.

We can't have any more contact with this troublemaker whoever he is shadows

next time

we must alert the authorities.

At all costs our family must stick together.

The Strike

Alarmed as they tried to imagine this stranger's purpose the kitchen swirled with smoke. Again and again they wondered where he was now in the darkness they must unite to eliminate this threat.

8

Chen Yun was cooking up a storm in Little Xu's kitchen frying pork slithers beyond the window skies dark. His fingers stirred in three green chilies spitting and wriggling in peanut oil they had just made love.

His lover called out to him softly above unknowable city crevasses stars glowing. Her beauty was rare as a streaking comet thinking about it his hands were burning from the chilies. He held them under the tap just a few months ago making this very dish for his wife and daughter. Maybe if he'd done that more often within her dimly lit flat barely discernible densities of night.

Where are you?

When he thought of his daughter, it was like his heart was locked in a tomb shadows papering the walls. Last summer after they left he felt numb in the water his fingers looked shriveled. Sometimes their faces seemed a blur through the high window trees rattled restlessly drifting back to the bedroom.

I'm lonely without you, baby.

Little Xu was a slip of warmth above the covers the nearest stars light years away. With loving affection he snaked a hand along her slim side you could never reach the end of time. He followed the teasing form of her decades lost between buttock ridges a bruised dark birthmark.

Are you glad that I'm here?

Last night they had called on Young Zhou the son of union chief Zhou Anguo in darkness the galaxy depleting its gaseous content.

The Strike

Young Zhou claimed his dad had just come out of hospital for some reason tension in the air. For three hours they waited in the Zhou's dimly lit kitchen while stars formed of the densest regions. The man's wife appeared angry at times fuelled by an interstellar medium of gas and dust.

They gave up eventually and left in a snow flurry a three wheeled cart took Chen Yun alone to his hotel to wait for news. He lay awake in multiple phases thinking of Little Xu strangely comforting distinguished by temperature and density. All night she had stayed around in hot diffuse regions not daring to sleep he finally ordered beer replenishing with matter and energy.

The next day in his room a continuous stream of particles still flowing outwards from the sun he decided to visit Little Xu's place. As he put on a new shirt the third floor aunty appeared with a hot flask stripping away the atmosphere of planets. For at least one hour he sat in his room a mosquito hovered interacting with the interstellar medium.

Chen Yun couldn't know that in one past life the third floor aunty was a maid serving a large aristocratic family the human costs quite ruinous. After the young master possessed her a second time in the garden giving birth she was promoted to third concubine. The young master never spoke to her again in a search for affection she wandered eternally through inner courtyards.

I'm going now.

After he'd rung several times sleepy Little Xu opened the door in a black sleeveless t-shirt on the twenty-third floor an irruption of light. He entered her passageway and went to the living room with a nervous smile Little Xu joining him on the brown sofa. Although he was passing the middle of his life no one would ever find them this high in the sky.

They chatted for a while Little Xu's teasing eyes eventually seeming delighted to see him throughout life he'd made malodorous mistakes. She said she hadn't been up long since last night so busy Chen Yun danced above the grave of his past.

The Strike

A little later Little Xu fetched black dice red cups stamped with a happiness logo his wife and daughter seemed so far away. She taught him to bet shaking the dice inside rattling cups heart still numb. He'd never played this he supposed her teasing laugh meant the wound would heal eventually.

She cheekily suggested they take something off as a forfeit after losing a trick the wind whistling around the upper floors of the building. He'd read about games like this before but never dreamed he might not see his family again.

The first game when he lost on purpose both knew dark galaxies common in the early stages of the universe. Later they kissed whenever opportunities arose surfaces bombarded. She whispered about being gentle the first time storms raging around her magnetic core. In the end there was no awkwardness during coronal mass ejections holding his hand very tight.

Chen Yun let himself be guided by her lying beneath as if in a dream their rhythm taking on the soft sofa. After a while their polarity flipped and Little Xu ascended trailing a small pale plasma tail. As they made love she appeared a deity skimming high above the mess of life ghosts calling his name within interstellar clouds.

So damn beautiful.

She was Xu Yue oddly enough you could never tell what on earth the future held. After that first night in the Northeastern Hotel she hadn't thought much of him although the flat felt too warm. Life was full of twists and turns where Chen Yun's hand had brushed along her leg now this irritating itchy sting.

During her time at the Happiness Bar older men in particular often surprised her with their passion the window frames rattling. They were fun in a way those months playing dice with drunk playboys after midnight she felt the soul of the city enter her.

Don't do that.

The wallet scam was all because of head barman Zhang Rong she preferred to sleep with her curtains open. Zhang Rong squatting while she flirted with customers city lights entered lifting their wallets. She felt bad although they were never caught the lights feeling like protection. If she refused Zhang Rong threatened her sometimes longing to return to her village.

She remembered summers when young their village was at the foot of a steep hill. She'd help his father push their cart of melons all the way to the market town each week money tight. Sometimes he'd let Xu Yue ride on the cart passing yellow fields they'd cut open the melons. They'd cut open the melons the knife hanging from his waist gave her a warm loving feeling. Starting and stopping the sun streaming down the fields to reach the market in the endless town.

ii.

She knew nothing about her new lover Xu Yue thought dimly moon close by. As they lay there Chen Yun rubbed her thigh distantly stinging. It could be easier to have an older man care for you like a father she was often helpless. Chen Yun massaged her shoulders now with strong hands the weight of the world pressing down.

Have you had a lot of women?

He tidied the apartment afterwards so patiently all her life she'd waited for someone who would love her more than her birth mother. She sometimes imagined all her romantic relationships as a ball of thread to be untangled before happiness came suffering first. You didn't need to know much about people really the snake wine finished.

What are you thinking?

He was Chen Yun caressed her back home after the pit strike started to avoid the authorities he and his boss Old Wang staying with different families each night hardly sleeping. Looking back their town had seemed to be waiting for the whole world to collapse without knowing it the very air poisoned. After decades of being in decline mah-jong tiles clicking and flying they longed for release smoke and steam from history's tomb.

Nothing.

Nights while the pits were closed he and Old Wang and the other union cadres often ended up at West Bar a storm of shells and fishbones before going to one of the small rooms. Sat amid velvet couches and large speakers cigarettes beer fruit and small cakes brought by lacquered hostesses were laid on the table. Old Wang loved to talk wildly while hostesses kept them company in their blue dresses full stomach curves.

Good, good, very tasty.

The card games could keep going for hours drinking themselves stupid. Old Wang was the worst after a few bottles singing raucous ballads the red-velvet walls trembled. Sometimes Chen Yun took one of the hostesses upstairs himself stuffing fifty in her hands later the place shut down. To be fair the strike hit their business hard because Little Xu young enough he wanted to look after her.

At the high tide of their passion he remembered the red glow that afternoon a suicide cliff of apartments. Somehow he'd been sure it was hers though no red bulb burned tonight light shone through the anonymous window frame.

I'm dying.

She was Xu Yue gripping her client's hand below feeling agony now where he touched her unthinkingly with his chili-tainted hands. The pain would last forever with her suffering she remembered that Chen Yun was married. While Chen Yun massaged her spine to make her better she decided to ask a few questions stinging voice.

Why aren't you with your wife and children?

She'd just assumed like most men there was no end to the pain. Suddenly disgust shook her as they drew apart he was bad just like so many others.

They're gone, gone.

The Strike

His voice seemed to come from far away over the years Xu Yue stormed to the bathroom despairing of this existence to rinse herself.

Walked out on me, didn't they.

After she'd squeezed wads of tissue dripping down herself she felt better. Hearing his sadness moon rose beyond the window night full of mysteries. Anyway they both had pasts letting slip the paper into the toilet full of loss and waste. Such being the nature of life she sighed it was the future everyone pinned their hopes on.

Hungry?

But Xu Yue didn't feel like eating now the darkness called. She wanted to walk outside holding Chen Yun's hand as a real city dweller new scenes to explore. She imagined being with him in one of those bars on West Peace Road clever young students playing the finger game.

Let's go somewhere.

A three wheel cab waited outside in no time the driver perched in the plastic screened box wearing a furry flying hat and goggles to protect from the wind they flew along. Screaming through the sun electricity lines coiling plastic sheets sealing Chen Yun put his hand on her knee.

Do you love me, Little Xu?

Her silence told him that he'd asked this too soon washing hanging from a cold balcony. The words froze on his lips as they sped on their bodies blasting with vibrations. By now he should know love disappeared if you talked about it too much desolate winter evening closing in. There probably wasn't much affection during this person's childhood in the countryside winters lasted forever.

They got out of the three wheeled cab downtown perhaps because of the strike few people. She surprisingly held his hand as they wandered along dark empty streets the questions kept coming.

Is the town staying together?

She was Little Xu wondering what was so exciting about the row at Bright Moon his hand drifted across her back. In her world if shit didn't concern you there came a stark pulse of beating drums.

He was Chen Yun as they heard the drums it was clear they were nearing People's Square space the cold wind slashing their eyes. Through the sub-zero temperatures of the night Little Xu held his hand unimaginably distant stars guiding them towards the dead centre. In the haunted streets uncanny shadows flickered tonight history itself on the march.

They approached the perimeter of the square silently a solemn line of soldiers confronted them. Somewhere in the formless space beyond them protestors lit fires almost in a trance Chen Yun released Little Xu's hand. The strikers sung an eerie song to the beating drums in a drowned sea of shadows soldiers staring them down.

Flames smouldered and faces in that cold space memories of the pit overwhelming Chen Yun the soldiers gestured with their guns to move on.

Scram. You can't stay here.

They walked quickly away in the shadows Chen Yun grew thoughtful. History had infected this empty borderland for centuries Old Wang talking of everyone going south. Now perhaps he understood his old boss's sense in this ghostly northern wilderness Little Xu rushing on angrily ahead of him.

iii.

Trying to keep up Chen Yun hurried down a lamp lit street for some reason Little Xu didn't wait. There were thousands of cities like this he might hide from his fate forever flowing on inside her black down coat.

Stop?

Some way ahead of him now in her green bobble hat Little Xu belonged to a different generation. She finally relented and Chen Yun almost caught up with her when he saw a crowd bunched in the light of a doorway snow falling again.

Starting soon, starting soon.

A tall actor pouted in the bright doorway everyone stared as if bewitched. She wore dark fishnet stockings and a red basque this winter evening crowd swelling in the cold air. Her painted face gleamed strangely in his sight Little Xu returning through the crowd.

What is it?

The tall woman stood in the doorway her bare legs and pale skin flickering with snow. This dark night passing she blew kisses like in a dream he'd never seen anything like it.

What the hell is this?

There was a notice apparently a show would start in a few minutes the crowd already doubling. He didn't know why this place intrigued him so much music drifting down the staircase magnetically he almost dragged Little Xu inside.

Let's go and see.

The actor seemed to be from another universe they ascended the narrow staircase beyond windows a snowstorm billowing. The highest floor opened into a dimly lit bar packed with smoking workers Chen Yun's head spun. Seats squashed together in a narrow gallery after buying tickets Little Xu's youthful figure stood out amid male drabness. Their seats overlooked a small stage area enveloped by thick fumes he wondered whether this was a political meeting. Little Xu lit a cigarette through her tightening silence he sensed her anger growing.

What have I done?

She was Xu Yue the other night on Yanan Road an old woman fell from her motorbike helpless like a cockroach on her back prickling sweat. Although the cars just kept driving around her Xu Yue didn't dare get involved in a stranger's affairs from bitter experience Chen Yun's instincts disturbed her. He'd dragged them into this peculiar place for some reason the crowd was waiting expectantly.

The Strike

Hello darlings.

Later flashing lights swept the floor amid a low murmur of voices the actor from the staircase appeared in a sparkly costume. Strobes played on her long white face and red lips faintly the night turning.

Don't be shy darlings.

The woman taunted them as she strutted to disco throbs the spectators shrank from this apparition. She displayed herself while the music blared Chen Yun trying to hear what she said.

They're real you know.

It dawned on Chen Yun in their small world they'd never seen anyone like this music both happy and sad. This borderland was where people learned who they were from history a low shudder of anticipation running through them.

I'm between lives, darlings.

He half expected this honest crowd might reject such transgression smoke rising to the gallery hard to breathe. Without any reserve going to each table in turn she called on anyone who dared to touch her the men kept smoking. She'd not one iota of awkwardness flaunting with ease everyone just sat there.

She introduced herself as Audrey from a faraway land as none dared speak her poise was striking.

I'm all me, nothing to hide.

With apparent stoicism the blue collar workers kept smoking this outsider another insult to be endured. He felt both intrigued and disturbed by her wondering why she went unchallenged it could be others too hungered for something new.

I don't feel safe here.

Little Xu stood abruptly he followed her down the narrow staircase from the gallery they must leave across the small stage area.

Something pressing, darlings?

As they appeared the actor seized on them in front of everyone face exposed playing to the gallery

    I hope I haven't disappointed you?

    He searched in vain for a comeback as they reached the door the strangeness of this day would last forever

    hearing her say

    They must be hot for each other

    a blast of laughter.

    He supposed the place where this figure came from was far far beyond his imagination

    discontinuity

The Strike

9

She was Audrey outside the Nine Dragons Bar night sun rolled hot over the red and orange dresses of the Yellow Cat girls opposite. Clouds of moonseed smoke hung thick above the bar a neon sign jerking off moist kisses.

He had dreamed often of returning food perfume sewage smells filling the bar street as Yellow Cat greeters Ott and Nott touted for business. Everything seemed as before Ott in velvet gold Nott in silver black giggling beyond with ghosts roaming hands.

Tight within their cheongsams nothing betrayed their former selves confusion after the police raid Joan barring him from Yellow Cat forever.

Outside Yellow Cat hostesses paraded in yellow and orange florals wiggling hips and batting lashes at blue-suited ghosts already half off their heads. Confused she thought this was the world where you could be different from one day to the next the show never ending.

Suddenly he forgot remembered how they'd all shot up in the dingy flats across the road whitehotcold coldhotwhite rushed by afterwards Ott was sick down her front it flowed back to her drifting stain still alive on her dress damning evidence he tried to scrape off redwhite until giving up. She was surprised because he remembered giving that dress to Ott a long time ago winning this talent show at the coast so hot his head spun almost blanking out.

All night crawled along the street hustlers of every variety calling people inside the bars after a while she saw two familiar faces he was terrified the ghosts would recognise her though he'd done nothing moon eyes they evaporated into smoke the music continuing dark matter they looked back and laughed probably friends of Joan. He was exiled now from Yellow Cat unable to find his way home that night the bar street cried for all that was lost. There was Joan star-spangled singing on the counter edge their eyes meeting she turned away in disgust apparently her bar thriving still He always liked it here, drifting amid starfields, wishing he hadn't made such a fucking mess of her life.

There was a scene outside Yellow Cat a few of the ghosts in blue flying over to where Ott and Nott were grabbing at them before long saying they'd taken money from one of their wallets fireflies fizzing around the bar lights the wallet appeared white in the smoke no one sure how much there'd been. As time passed everything got heated eyes glaring throats bulging Ott and Nott swung their handbags round chairs flying a blue ghost seized Nott by the throat a sound like metal tearing her ghost sprang up to help her he realized Joan was watching from inside the bar. Her eyes burned husky voice yellow hair as he'd rebelled that final time she banished her into the wilderness of a faraway land.

He ignored her and went to help Ott a few seconds later the ghosts in blue blocking the way she shoved with his fingers Ott and Nott chanting we will kill you with love their ghosts advanced still demanding the fifty dollars he defended his friends saying we belong here the ghosts howling and Nott sick across the universe she moved aside. Although he'd never seen them before a few cops who worked the street wanted to know what the fuss was at that moment as the ghosts blustered about the fifty dollars she said it was me

the one you want is me.

He felt Nott and Ott's gratitude for this sacrifice saying he was the guilty one. She'd stood for his old friends as the crowd closed round too late seeing Joan laugh behind a hand tattooed with death a trap she was close with these cops.

The whole night rolled through the street expanding and sucking up flotsam and jetsam as they advanced towards the cop shop a few hundred metres away the crowd swelling with punters and drinkers from other bars bawling from tables others joining a twisting screwing mob of screaming fighting junkies hookers pushers under a smog-grilled sun choking inside dark blue haze they were an army for a laugh with snake smokes legs skirts make-up nausea.

Spilling through the cop shop door he was surprised to see the same bunch of ghosts from the street earlier dressed as cops alarms blaring she realised the cop shop was located inside one of the oldest bars hardly anyone would know flagons of snake stashed on a filthy shelf a few cops watching Ott Nott pounding a ghost's head on the floor for quite some time he wanted to apologise to everyone.

At last the cop boss asked who was guilty to their surprise Joan stepped forward for ages he hadn't seen her until the crowd gasped as she shook her fist and rasped in her low angry voice this dude was barred

this loser shouldn't be here.

The cop asked was she guilty or not thanks to Julie the crowd shouting

he couldn't deny anything.

The cop boss used a stick to gently raise his skirt underneath orange panties when she looked the chamber echoing with screams one of the girls had a knife from her bag it came out whistling and fighting he guessed it was Nott after stabbing one of the ghosts being dragged forward to the place he'd been before.

The captain asked her intentions from the corner of her mouth Ott saying get the hell out now everyone distracted they made for the door furtively the cop boss asking for the stolen money before stars fuzzing over they were allowed to go.

As they walked Nott warned watch out her dress still pulled up above his waist everything hanging out.

No one seemed to notice passing a shuttered liquor store hands reaching through he craved something else after all that sitting outside

The Strike

Nine Dragons watching the Yellow Cat hostesses opposite as if nothing had happened Nott ordering snake she couldn't remember a damn thing.

Night fell across the bar street ghosts joining the Yellow Cat hostesses all over them once again excluded she felt the need to get out of his head hearing a ghost ask to score some gear Nott and Ott saw a chance to work a scam her arm had the pale skin of a user.

The hostesses pressed the ghost for cash in the confusion he claimed he hadn't wanted anything threatening him Ott opened her handbag apparently she was the one with the knife the ghost struggling against the two hostesses blocking his way amid universal entropy he was dead.

The ghost walked somberly to the back of the bar up the stairs to the rooms heart racing following him into the room although it was some time later they finally had the junk as gaunt white arms shot up under the bed a picturebook of images before and after she felt shocked and very sick dark clouds crawling through a door and lying on a red bed he remembered never being there.

The ghost entered moments later she felt many arms holding him down her legs cold with a frightening passion faces names history rushing through the window in a wet stream released forever

opening his eyes in the grey dawn light the boy from the theatre dressing at the window with a jarring sadness he remembered where she was now that world lost forever he could never go back

discontinuity.

The Strike

10

She was Mrs Zhang cleaning the fridge in the year of the horse Old
Yu appeared from their bedroom in a long grey coat and slippers. She
worried as he changed this cold afternoon they'd be parted forever in
the icy draft from the door.

You're going?

Yeah he said a black scarf knotted around his neck

today his usual theatre day.

She felt hurt by that misdirection afterwards he unlocked the door
then went down the stairs.

I won't be long.

Old Yu hurried through the courtyard snug in his wool hat the sun
shimmied through the afternoon. A scrawny cat hung around the
dustbins tangled with burned out firecracker strings he slipped
through the gate. Not far along Zhongshan Road he caught a bus
towards the past. He sat alone by the window as a blue coated
attendant checked his ticket unsettled clouds drifted through a
strangely unfamiliar sky.

Right you are, Grandpa.

Old Yu's bus was passing the shuttered timber works where he
slaved for many cold winters a man standing outside with a dog. He'd
take his daughter to the timber baths once a week there was talk of
investors developing the rest of the site as the supermarket so popular
nothing decided.

What going on, driver?

He'd given his youth to the timber works because of the strike the bus took a different route. Fuxing Road was closed as far as the eye could see whole estates stranded beyond.

It's been days now.

Days, which became years.

At the turn of the last century his grandparents sold their cow and moved north to this city for work they crossed Chunfeng Road. The bus gears groaned long ago he once saw sepia snaps of faded faces from that time. Today the Northern Star supermarket served the surrounding estates full of unemployed timber workers a stray balloon bobbled above the car park.

Where will it stop?

Often he and his wife Jiahui wandered through the supermarket aisles bright with promotions there was writing on the fluttering red balloon. The brightly packaged goods seemed like seeds of a new era forming miles to the south they usually went home with friend chicken. She still preferred the wet market above the Long Peace Primary School the balloon changed course abruptly drifting towards the old rail depot.

They were the future once strange to say he more or less knew where he was going. They passed blackened former workshop buildings where he'd been placed for twenty years of his life under a timber sky stuck behind a road gritter.

Number One Timber Factory. Building the Nation.

He sometimes wondered who the hell he'd been in the past the bus overtook the gritter or might have before braking too late at the entrance to the bus station.

At the long distance bus terminal a young man steadied him on the bus steps hawkers surging with bags of dried fish. He seldom went far these days sinking onto a hard metal seat the black-and-white monitor instantly started up with a cantonese movie.

The bendy bus took forever to turn out of the garage because of heavy traffic pressure building in his chest. The town had been promising to build a new bus station for years after Guihua's arrest he'd no idea what had happened to her. Finally the driver made a break for it somewhere in Five Colour Valley he knew she had a deer farm.

After returning from the countryside married to Jiahui he thought he might run into Guihua on the street endless construction. Although he never did new snowfall covered the dirt unexpectedly instead he met her farmer husband. That afternoon before Dongmei started middle school they were at Happy Future buying her uniform the orange sun seeped through a gray cloud. Stood with Dongmei at the counter birds swooping from snowy hills a craggy country man talked to the cashier. Out of nowhere he heard the man say Guihua's name and then

My wife was brought up in the town.

The farmer looked older than Guihua quite often he feared how hungry birds got in winter. He was holding a child's hand the creatures circled the bus as they left downtown. Old Yu found the girl hard to take in for a moment feeling giddy the road twisted and turned. She was evidence of lost years since that fatal summer slipping out to fetch food the bus roaring across a ditch.

We have a deer farm out at Five Colour Valley.

After that encounter making inquiries in the timber works he learned Guihua returned at least five years ago the sun slipping out from a labour camp in the White Snow Mountains. He had trouble sleeping because of the strange knowledge that Guihua also had a daughter rats getting at their bins lately. Slowly screaming wheels they climbed the sky stretching for miles across the afternoon of small thickets and hills. Out here with the distant sun in this desolate land his breath froze. Sadness outlasted humans as they stuttered along an unfinished road.

You couldn't see anyone for miles emptiness erased small people such as them.

Ten fords village.

Near this smoky village was that farm where Ma and Pa were sent to be reformed through hard labour their bus clanking and groaning. They passed gates with firewood stacked neatly Pa never recovered from their ordeal while Ma seldom went outside frostbite taking four of her toes.

Still everyone suffered in those days the bus moving towards the crest of the hill at least his grandparents were old party members while Guihua's family were suspect for their shop.

We're giving you a chance, little troublemaker, because of your parents.

Without such favourable treatment galaxies on the other hand might he have found the courage to defend her beyond the glass snowdrifts. Since the army took her that night he'd tortured himself pointlessly snow piling ten feet deep.

He stared at the lines of trees and hedges etched across the hills birds fluttering and diving. They engraved a suppressed history that enemies had dug and tunnelled throughout the land thousands dead. After those demons gave up disgusting secrets were discovered down there in their bases a kind of bloody hell. Some had stayed underground for months poison gas and disease finally taking their toll.

History had ravaged this wasteland from the start the conductor shouting to the driver. Yet he could never quite see it as belonging to him the bus slowed down.

You get out here, Grandpa.

The driver pointed up the road full of uncertainty it forked right into a space blank as the river where he wrote poems in the morning. The bus moved away down the hill in a puff of smoke was it really possible to blow away the past.

Reaching the top gasping for breath the sky opened down to his right a long thin farm building. The bus's engine faded into nothing on the icy hill he tried not to slip. He saw himself as a poisonous arrow deep snow hedgerow aimed right at her heart.

Someone moved down there had to be life. There was a kind of

The Strike

cattle pen flickering through snow it appeared a barren place from that distance.

He descended ever closer to their farm on the bleak hill trouser legs sopping damp below his long grey coat. His chest and arms were deep frozen inside this snowfilled afternoon remorse a few wild birds flapped overhead. He thought he saw a woman pouring water from a bucket in this life you shouldn't return. She probably hadn't seen yet as he went on down feeling it must be her.

He remembered Guihua wearing her green army uniform that day of her disappearance inside a black hole atmosphere of menace.

You mustn't worry, brother.

He thought those were the last words she'd said as they arrested her the bus had quickly vanished. She told him not to worry later the bus would come back this way. What if there was no other world after death a large gate at the bottom a yard beyond where mistakes forgiven.

Mustn't worry.

This winter day deep as a sea she would be scared by this drifting ghost. Should the bus return now quite gladly he would leave here. Had they embraced one last time before the soldiers took her near the factory gates surely by now she would have noticed him.

You mustn't.

He sighed of course that hadn't been last time when he said last time what he meant was last time ever sleepless before the last time.

Foul weed.

Her small body shaking from blows and kicks on that bench in the factory yard she refused to speak. Angry fists of their enemies waved in the air blank shouts echoing across the night.

At least they hadn't forced him to strike her before the sky caved in he'd already written that letter accusing her. Each work team sent representatives forward to abuse her physically the endless snow made him despair. She gave him a peculiar look as they finally dragged her away to make herself unforgettable a frozen bird dropped

88

like a stone.

See troublemaker, your lover has written these words.

The woman approached the gate with that face he would remember for as long as dark emptiness struck the earth from space.

Hello.

She stood a few feet away all of us made from dust of stars. He had a black heart she knew this world still went round the sun. Guihua seemed hardly changed from decades ago bright eyes red cheeks near as before. She swung in her long coat on the lowest bar of the gate as the years rolled away he became puzzled. After several moments sun streaked thinly through a cloud gap revelation glimmered.

I think I'm looking for your mother.

This was a girl's fresh bright face framed by fur her coat dolphin silver. Of course this must be the daughter from the store all those summers ago a strong urge to smoke a cigarette.

I'm Chunyan, her daughter.

Her smile curious she said I saw you in the snow up there

she looked so like Guihua.

At the same time his memory wasn't reliable as far as he knew she couldn't guess.

She invited him to come in saying Ma will be back soon

she was perhaps a bit taller.

She told him that her mother was visiting a neighbour of course it had to be remembered

he was old now.

He followed more calmly because Guihua wasn't there the yard smelled of animal shit. Suspecting nothing the girl led the way as they passed a fat cat scratching on a brick wall she asked him questions.

I'm an old friend of your ma's.

Their voices sounded thin in this open space he didn't belong. He was just passing through he murmured unconvincing as this would sound

everyone was.

The Strike

She didn't press him for details walking across the yard towards their little brick house he swallowed repeatedly. In the yard he noticed a white outbuilding with a low corrugated roof that morning Jiahui felt uncomfortable. The girl said charmingly would Uncle like her to see around the farm if he wasn't too tired

he worried about his wife's health.

The girl led him behind that white building swaying trees Jiahui suffered from faintness.

They saw a cow lying on the ground by a winter wall of hay there was dry blood. Twenty years ago Guihua cut her finger while peeling an apple he sucked it.

Several calves crowded around her udders he remembered the blood soaking through like truth.

You've known Ma a long time then?

Yes he said stepping across frozen mud urine there was a smell of life and death.

Somehow he felt this was trespass as she led him towards the deer pens under that coat she might even look much like Guihua. His family had nothing as good as this farmyard buried under deep snow she must sometimes have thought of him.

There's twenty of them at the moment.

The deer were so vulnerable standing in their pen he needed badly to piss. They looked like old men numbly caged his bladder was weak these days. In their frozen faces seemed to be a reflection of Guihua's traumatized expression fifteen or twenty times a day he had to piss. They were fond of their porcelain inside toilet after years of going outdoors he cleaned it every day.

Shall we go in the house?

She was Sun Chunyan stung by the wind from the bleak hills. The sun had disappeared behind some clouds strange this old man should just appear like this with Ma away in town.

This is our home.

There was still that slight feeling of loss opening the door of their house where Pa had died just yesterday it seemed the deer were hungry.

She was a freshman student she said watching him stamp his feet for ages to lose the cold

from the door.

Right now she was home for new year through the door to the past this hill farm where her life had started with Ma and Pa they were a family.

She showed the old man inside the hut her father always loved taking her for hikes. Sitting him on the brick kang where she and Ma slept there hadn't been as many visitors after father died she removed his coat. Her boyfriend was going to call soon on the way from Hebin their lives might be about to change forever.

Ma should be here soon.

Ma had promised to come home early to meet her boyfriend for the first time their house struck her as simple and even poor. She sensed Ma didn't like the idea of her having a boyfriend because of something bad that happened in her past the old man sneezed. His arrival felt like a welcome diversion although still unexplained there was a crack in the window.

Let me get you something to drink.

Once before when she tried to introduce Ma to a boyfriend in the kitchen fetching hot water the stranger seemed strangely emotional. When she returned he was studying a framed photograph on the scratched dresser sitting opposite. He stared quietly at the portrait of her mother still elegant and beautiful one of their cats was mewing pathetically to come in.

Excuse me, is this Xia Guihua?

Yes she said surprised late afternoon sun probing his face because she thought they'd known each other.

He touched the photograph almost respectfully removing her thick padded coat. A strange note entered his voice when a tawny cat leaped up on the outside windowledge she offered him food.

The Strike

I don't want to cause trouble.

Chunyan said they would grill meat tonight anyway her boyfriend surely starving after a long bus journey. She went to the outer room where their grill sat atop a brick kiln her earliest memories were of Pa cooking while alive.

I'm not worth it.

He was Old Yu sat on the kang the world looking at Guihua's face for the first time in years the past dissolved. She had a middle aged rueful smile in those gentle lines was written endless suffering. This familiar but strange face opened and closed like in his dreams he wanted to talk to her.

Don't worry.

The young woman abused in that factory yard was somewhere inside here the earth shook. What happened that long ago day had set her on her path to this hut for better or worse the snow piled high outside.

Her face was a clock.

Her face was a clock that wouldn't stop ticking. Her face was a clock that couldn't go back. Her face was a clock otherwise all her blessings and sadness would have been different.

Her face was gunfire on a deathly night. Her face was bodies floating on the river. Her face was fear a stranger might come by at any moment.

Her face was a clock stopped by him

Seconds he didn't belong here. Seconds the table cloth was torn. Seconds seconds the chair leg was broken. Seconds seconds their clothes were folded on wood shelves.

Your mother must have suffered.

She'd returned silently shadows scouring the hill with a plate of grilled deer meat. She gave him some through the gloom outside callous birds swooped asking did you ever meet
my father.

He felt nervous Guihua might return soon full night would find him sat on her bed. Although he tried to eat the light was fast fading this late winter afternoon.

Not bad.

We were happy the three of us she told him softly Pa died last year.

When I knew your mother he said queasy with foreboding
she hadn't met your father yet.

Well she said wondering about this shy man
you go back a long way don't you.

Your ma suffered so much he sighed without realising she was listening to her family's enemy.

Well I think everyone suffered she said whispering those times are hard for my generation to understand.

Do you have a boyfriend?

Actually she laughed for a moment leaning forward
we're expecting him any moment.

He saw a resemblance to Guihua because the world was younger now his voice sounded emotional.

Is your boyfriend good to you?

She helped him lie on the kang blood rushed to his head which he supposed Guihua and her husband had shared for years. Sweetly she suggested that he rest for a few minutes her face looked concerned. She acted with kindness he hoped she would find someone better loosening his belt. He felt her soft leg make contact as they lay side by side the moon rose beyond the window. They held hands peacefully for several minutes he thought how her father filled this space.

Their anxieties subsided as they rested there mutual stillness waiting for the absent he drifted in comforting memories. Gradually he felt pressure grow in his bladder a mobile rang.

That might be your boyfriend now.

Yes she said the phone ringing next door you'll meet him soon.

Quickly she got up thinking what if something bad had happened to her boyfriend Chunjiang now the floor felt damn cold as he followed desperate to relieve himself the moon visible through thin night clouds. There was no toilet in the house the smell of grilled meat everywhere he'd have to put on his boots and go out. On the phone she was asking someone where are you while he tied his boots he wasn't sure whether it was her boyfriend

he opened the door.

I won't be long.

There wasn't much cover in the yard he relieved himself. The sky was so low that he slunk shyly behind the barn a cow chewed on its hay.

His piss dribbled on this icy hard ground he didn't belong. At the same time the wind ripped through his trousers a cat stalked nastily along the hedgerow. What was he doing on this hill under an unfamiliar night sky the piss trickled accusingly back towards him.

He shook himself with clumsy hands suddenly it was obvious he'd made a big mistake. Dark birds flew through the cold shadows he started to walk towards the gate.

All these years close to the hedge it was as if he'd thought there was an alternative life waiting for him. Sometimes keeping his head low that other life had seemed more fucking real than his life with his family. Those two existences had been parallel paths on a winter hillside when he glanced back there was the new girl's silhouette in the window.

He went through the gate and then shut it while the early stars disappeared behind a cloud.

They would never meet again now he trudged up the road away from the farm. He pressed on in this night wilderness the decision to leave seemed the sensible one. The ridge of the hill was dimly visible for want of anything better people always said that he kept his feet on the ground.

Yet he'd secretly treasured the memory of Guihua when it would have been more realistic to move on his boots were damp.

Hadn't his behaviour been seriously strange for years acting

The Strike

detached from life while Jiahui repaired cookers and sewed patches on his overalls. He'd been a loser all along his boots slipped and slid crazily as a father and husband.

From out of nowhere a large car approached in this dark night he thought it had to be her returning. The engine noise got louder without knowing why he dropped into the snowy ditch at the side of the road his grave.

Wasn't it strange that he should make himself invisible after coming all this way to see her in the wet and cold he sank low.

He pressed himself ever flatter as a shadow appeared at the top of the road his heart raced. Snow was everywhere inside his damn clothes he saw a white van coming down.

Long after he was sure it had continued past the farm he climbed out inside his soaked shirt. There was a pain in his chest he made for the bus stop at the top of the hill. His absence would have worried Jiahui by now a bird or animal made a noise in the hedgerow.

All these years he'd failed to give her the love she deserved a steep drop into a pothole. Now he was lost in this wilderness there wouldn't be any more buses.

He probably wouldn't survive this night the temperature would drop. No more buses would come so far as he knew in his life he'd achieved nothing. The top of the hill didn't look any closer for whatever reason young people had dreams.

He blamed their times running out of breath because history had put the squeeze on many of his generation. He remembered watching the sun rise one long ago afternoon people longed to be significant.

Pain ambushed him finally on the empty road his breath sounded rasping. Jiahui always asked him to accompany her for exercises in the mornings some people just preferred writing and being alone. The key moments of this life flashed before his eyes it must be death had prepared this ambush. He would pass up here without apologising to his wife and daughter his wet clothes stuck to his body. His daughter down south had no one to care for her like Guihua's child

95

on the twilight hill the dark lines of hedges and copses like writing. He froze all those embankment mornings his words fading.

Thereafter Old Yu sat there words twigs trunks silently remembering his daughter. Sometimes afterwards moon earth a bus came along the road. When it had almost gone past a dark blue metal shadow in the shadows the conductor called for the driver to stop a petrol stink inside.

Old Yu stood in the dark the door miraculously opened. She was the conductor sensed at once that he needed help because his face was very pale he could hardly come up the steps shivering with her hand on his shoulder.

Take me back.

Shortly before Six Brooks Valley driving slowly down the steep hill after letting on one more there was a shout from the back she was chatting to the driver because the old grandfather had fallen suddenly from his seat and was lying flat and distressed on the floor of the bus she came running with her ticket machine.

11

He was Sun Tiankong jogging backwards along the main road east through the railcar estate setting sun in his eyes. The whole estate was simply known as railcar on the far side of town the planners built schools even a hospital. His fifty-seven year old feet looped the closed gas station with a steady rhythm frozen sparrows dropping from the sky. Small piles of cardboard smouldered at intervals slagheaps of snow marked the level roadside.

Sun Tiankong tried to maintain a speed between a run and a walk a large black sedan approached from behind. He dodged just in time the arrogant government motor nearly mangling his leg. What he lacked in mobility he made up for in hearing as he reached Old Zhang's supermarket exhaust drifted like breath across the road.

At Old Zhang's supermarket you could buy tinned food pausing for breath and nearly fresh vegetables. They were low on white vinegar and peanut oil although it was best to plan for emergencies dancing around a pile of steaming dog shit making do as always. He thought about asking Old Zhang for credit then decided against it grey clouds dulling the sun their family knew him. The Zhangs were laid off like the rest of them this side of new year no point in presuming on friendship.

He was tired from home swimming practice as usual that morning after his wife left for the community prize draw the VCD going on. His body extended beyond the end of their battered old sofa without the inconvenience of water raising and lowering his legs. Apparently some new brand of laundry powder was being given away to attract customers his sagging gut was supported by a cushion. His best years gone he was determined to learn new skills that might prepare him for cramps in his legs.

After swimming practice he lost little time getting to the pharmacy on Sundays their quiet estate of redundant railcar workers came alive. The little shop was heady with medicinal smells he met his former supervisor Old Lin. Together they negotiated a discount for a large bag of sugarless cereals on this estate the chance to save a few cents was valued.

While he and Old Lin traded tips about kidney tonics by the door was a table with leaflets promoting free blood pressure tests. Although Tiankong assumed his was high for a man this age the hem of the trousers came down again.

So far there hadn't been a moment to read the leaflets since the sky was an expectant white most likely it would snow again soon. While he'd nothing much to do since being laid off he was intent on self cultivation going steady on icy patches to be a better person in the future. Every month that passed the good old days welding railway cars felt more and more like they'd been lived by a stranger taken away in an ambulance. The noise of the workshop was what stayed with him in his ears the continual assault of body parts being hammered on the way home.

Just as he reached the front of the apartments on a tide of memory that bloody official car pulled up again. The car slowing a moment later a familiar figure emerged under a drab sky walking up and down stiffly. The guy clutched a parcel wrapped in gift paper Tiankong made himself small as he passed.

Hey, Brother Sun.

After the stranger disappeared into stairwell three Sun was spotted by his old sparring partner Wang Dianbo in a blue cap the block opposite always noisy. Sweeping snow with his wood brush even on the coldest days his cap was a constant sight for those in the estate with windows.

The Strike

Who was that big shot?

Sun Tiankong and Wang Dianbo had much in common a donkey cart went by piled high with scrap and many differences. Tiankong was laid off from the plant six months before Dianbo as it happened the sun went behind a cloud with the factory folding.

Dianbo now had a little business going in recycled paper collected from bins government support was thin.

Tiankong told his friend the stranger was none other than Suifen's mayor visiting police chief Pang Linfeng in staircase three a pack of magpies massing on a pylon. Linfeng's husband Tieguo had mentioned a few days ago a birthday party for their child he was collecting water money.

We don't see the mayor much around here

Tiankong agreed a rare sighting.

While Tiankong was something of a thinker in many people's eyes Dianbo carried on like a noisy nuisance. Sure enough Dianbo complained striking Bright Moon workers were getting all the sympathy earth freezing over

while railcar workers suffered more.

The Bright Moon workers were rewarded for making a stink he spat globulously

their own pensions years in arrears.

Now Mayor Ma himself showed up on their estate daringly Dianbo sensed the chance to deliver a message. He brandished his brush like a curse starting to scratch defiant words in the snow several months deep.

For all Tiankong's natural caution he couldn't help conceding since ancient times biting winds from the east a tradition of commoners petitioning nobs. Back then petitions were often hung from a pole outside the palace gate he sneezed violently.

As Dianbo scraped his message deep on the deep snow bank opposite staircase three Tiankong thought things through. The precise location of their message had implications he told Dianbo a hot water pipe melting the white stuff closer to the wall.

Did they anticipate the mayor glancing down at their words from the kitchen of Linfeng's apartment

clouds closely contained them.

Or was it more likely he would discover them when leaving they presumed his way would pass the bank

tonight could well be moonless.

Unsure which case was most probable while the afternoon slipped away they also scrapped about literary style. Tiankong argued for keeping things oblique brush swirling trailing dead leaves Dianbo took shot at the mayor's cultural level. Tiankong couldn't move him as the brush was in Dianbo's hands the temperature dropping fast.

Dog official!

This blunt message being scratched across the snow the odd couple retreated to Dianbo's apartment in the block opposite a smell of drains. The sun was sinking low by all signs they had little time left to make an impression. One option was to lure the mayor outside to read their message Dianbo opened a bottle of snake. On the other hand they could simply leave it as a statement buried in snow clinking glasses.

The right course of action depended on the personality of the mayor they allowed alcoholically important people were dangerous. Dianbo brandished a second bottle making wild claims which Tiankong parried in the style of their endless chinese chess games time

depleted fruitlessly.

Dianbo finally persuaded a half drunk Tiankong to visit that afternoon Pang Linfeng's apartment refilling glasses they were neighbours

in passing.

On the excuse of bringing birthday greetings for Pang Linfeng's son he said Tiankong could take the opportunity to size up the rotten mayor

if indeed he was.

The Strike

After the second bottle Dianbo upended an ash tray all over himself Tiankong had to lie down.

ii.

She was police chief Pang Linfeng this afternoon for her son's birthday their small home crowded. Her son Yugong raced around the guests on a sugar high conversations fizzing. While everyone looked cheerful she asked Aunty Zhu to follow her into their bedroom for a few minutes the floor unsteady beneath their feet.

You don't look well, Linfeng.

Aunty Zhu was a bulky wild eyed woman in her sixties this afternoon the bedroom tidier than usual. She came with a wrinkled fleshy face and dyed curly black hair trailing over her shoulders Linfeng shut the door softly.

It's the same problem, Aunty.

Linfeng told her she found it hard to sleep these nights comet debris flying through space.

Show me your hand.

Aunty Zhu was a traditional medicine doctor in their remote part of the universe old beliefs held sway. With warm fingers Aunty held Linfeng's wrist pulsating nova to make her diagnosis electric heater humming.

Your life force is being attacked.

Several lifetimes ago Pang Linfeng was second wife in an aristocratic household hundreds of maids to manage. Her housekeeping skills were much praised during one month long imperial visitation the costs appalling. Yet a small error in etiquette was ruinous in the end her entire family beheaded from top to bottom.

While Linfeng tried to breathe deeply Aunty Zhu massaged her neck and rambled softly about conjunctions of stars and planets.

The Strike

Linfeng couldn't forget that Mayor Ma was sitting next door Aunty urged her to dress warmly as long as she kept the cold out

she would defeat her enemies.

Which enemies Aunty, how can I know them?

They were massing on all sides Aunty Zhu claimed most likely wolf spirits.

Linfeng had been infuriated when damn mayor Ma Minsheng showed up earlier at Yugong's party burrowing into the warmth of Aunty's black sweater. She and the mayor were dragged to a meeting with Province Secretary Mao only that morning Yugong noisy in the living room. Secretary Mao asked her to lead an investigation into the maybe irregular sale of the Bright Moon plant even though this was her son's birthday he shouldn't get too wound up.

I'm tough, Aunty.

Linfeng left eventually to collect her thoughts in the kitchen Meizhu her sister in law was washing up broken glass.

She was Pan Meizhu feeling carefully for sharp shards in the murky water if the whispers about Mayor Ma and that sale were real a risky moment for Linfeng. Realising that her sister in law needed space to think because of her good intuition the sun going down outside.

OK, you take over sister.

She was Linfeng dropping glass in the bin that morning Secretary Mao's sly smile as he announced her new task still chilling. Although iron bum Mao they called him was a fool he'd neatly dumped this investigation into corruption at Bright Moon onto her the bin lid snapped shut.

Shit!

Since Secretary Mao probably knew that Mayor Ma took bribes from Boss Cui until pieces of broken glass still swirled like sharks in the dirty water. Success in life depended on relationships at the top head spinning she tried to sense her next move.

Minsheng is asking for you.

The Strike

Her husband Tieguo appeared outside the window sun bleeding over snowy buildings. Tieguo was laid off from his foreman's job at the railcar factory three years ago a shaving cut on his throat. They returned to the others in the next room the mayor pulled out a giftwrapped package.

Yugong, look, Mayor Ma has made a kind gesture.

As she thanked the mayor Linfeng was checking that there was nothing luxurious in their home to arouse suspicion most of the food already gone. Nearly all the top leaders lived in modest apartments although they had plenty of money perhaps they should have filled more dumplings.

Why don't you open Uncle Ma's present later?

Mayor Ma's frustrated look showed he hadn't been able to talk to her pointedly placing his gift on a side table. The mayor's frown deepened as Yugang puffed out the candles Tieguo preparing to take photos.

1, 2, 3, eggplant…

They smiled for the lens even after this with her arm around her son Linfeng still caught on her mounting problems. That devious Secretary Mao had sprung another surprise on her this morning camera flashing it seemed some fugitive from Hebin was at large in Suifen.

Immediately after being told this she called the police chief in Hebin Tieguo snapped away learning sun moon this troublemaker was some union man who'd recently fled. No one knew what he was doing in their town until facts were clear the repeated flashes made her headache flare. Mayor Ma might try and use this news against her after her husband finally had enough photos they all heard a ghostly tapping at the door.

Let me go.

The Strike

iii.

Pang Linfeng drew back the bolt unexpectedly carrying a box of apples the rumpled form of scruffy Old Sun coalesced in the shadows.

Old Sun collected the water and electricity dues on their staircase clothes soiled with cigarette ash she detected a pungent smell wafting in the air no choice but to take him inside.

Hey everyone, meet our neighbour, Old Sun.

He was Sun Tiankong had never been inside the police chief's apartment perhaps from nerves at once letting slip a fart as Linfeng led him into a full room. He'd met hardly anyone here unless he was mistaken the fart struck him as odourless. Pang Linfeng might be a police chief but there was nothing showy about the apartment's worn furniture much like his own the whole thing looking pretty dull.

I've come to congratulate the young master.

Pang Linfeng introduced him to members of her family and Mayor Ma who he saw earlier emerging from a black car at dusk gas clouds expanding through interstellar space.

Yes, why don't you sit here.

Sun Tiankong was already squeezing onto the sofa beside the cadaverous mayor a drab table sticky with newly poured beers. Mayor Ma's face radiated contempt even after a gulp for courage Tiankong wouldn't dare speak if not for the heating turned up very high.

We don't see you much round here.

He was Ma Minsheng considered himself a master of polite nothings although frustration was mounting in the warm room coughing dryly. Struggling to control his temper because false rumours about his arrest had weakened his authority this rude old man reeked of drink.

What do you do, Grandpa?

The mayor's choice of words irritated Tiankong as this puffed up little boss only looked a few years younger the room suddenly silent.

The Strike

Me? What do you think? I'm on the scrapheap like everyone else
here.
Tiankong explained in bursts that he hadn't received his pension
from the factory for six months to be fair
others were worse off.
You should meet my neighbor Dianbo hasn't been paid for nearly
one year.
Everyone was talking about the damn Bright Moon lot Tiankong
said why should railway car workers be ignored.
We did our bit for the country as well.
Yes murmured Aunty Zhu and one or two others for decades
turning out out railway carriages for the nation.
The government could rely on us in the past
where would anyone have got without railcars.
You couldn't go anywhere.
The spirit of rebellious Dianbo threatened to enter them in this
modest room of the estate
bitter proud memories glimmering in their eyes.
We fitted a hundred cars a week when I was foreman Tieguo
bragging
everyone pulled together.
We always had the best lantern display at festivals said Aunty
Wang
many toiled there for twenty years.
People came from other factories to see our lanterns five times
we won the excellent work unit prize.
Now what's happened to us?
The past is dead Tiankong said sweating
until we dropped
to build up the estate.
When the government said go we went there and if they said the
sky was grey on Sundays
we collected dead birds from the ground.

The Strike

We were proud of ourselves hammering out railway cars for the future you ask Zhang Tieguo
he's laid off as well.
What does he do but clean all day in our empty guest house.
We're all going through this together my friend.
He was Mayor Ma Minsheng believed he knew how to talk to common people in this outer spiral of the galaxy trouble easily flaring up. He figured he'd first control this situation drifting through stormy solar clouds this dodgy grandfather's background should be checked out later.
At his daughter's wedding last year he told them brightly they asked ordinary workers
as well as officials
to share their happiness all uniting.
We're in this together Mayor Ma declared with confidence
whatever our role people love this town.
The higher ups looks out for us
occasionally
progress slower than people would like.
They should take heart from their leaders' example although the past was lost
there would be expansion at an ever increasing rate.
Mayor Ma extended his glass through an invisible particle field electric light flickering around them Tiankong's glass tilted unsteadily.
Let's drink, old friend.
Tiankong's glass jerked at the last moment beer dripped down the mayor's gray wool sweater in the living room earth sun shocked silence.
It was an accident.
Linfeng took the mayor to the kitchen time unfroze saying Old Sun had never been asked in the first place his sweater wiped with a cloth.
Stupid old fool.

The Strike

Tieguo gave the mayor one of his shirts to wear in the murmuring
night Linfeng claimed rebellion was rare on their estate trees rattling
in the wind.

We have more serious problems to face.

He was Sun Tiankong couldn't believe what he'd done beers
tonight in the empty universe blood rushing to his head. He must flee
heart racing to find Dianbo and prevent disaster before it got worse
the door opening for him.

I'm sorry everyone.

Mayor Ma left the kitchen not long after that following him down
the stairwell Linfeng muttered apologies. He pressed on her again
dark within his knee length wool coat there were critical problems to
solve.

That fugitive from Hebin.

Cautiously she reflected it seemed a coincidence that troublemaker
Chen Yun turned up from nowhere this winter

the dingy space at the bottom of the stairs jammed with bicycles.

According to her enquiries in Hebin she said Chen was a union
man

rusty chains

before going on the run.

Although they should watch him there seemed no need

for alarm

extruding spokes

the stairwell cold.

You don't understand.

This was what Mayor Ma had been waiting all day to say by the
frozen bins at the bottom of the stairs

perceptions mattered.

Certain people wanted to blame these troubles on the sale of the
plant but an arrest in his view

leaking garbage

would show external factors were responsible.

The Strike

This opportunity mustn't be allowed to slip away through a cold doorway

bring him in quickly.

They should use this to their advantage afterwards dark reaching in this situation would be different.

Linfeng understood the mayor was proposing an alliance to save their necks his car drew up softly. She promised the arrest would happen as soon as possible in the swirling snow her boss would likely prevail in any power struggle.

The mayor's car drew away within the chill wind ice particles colliding she stayed and made a few calls to arrange things. Working her phone out of the corner of her eye she dimly perceived an old man raking in the shadows over and again brandishing a stick. Scratching over something in the snow dead leaves attached to a broom dragged across the windswept bank erasing whatever had been there forever.

The Strike

12

He was Pytor realized the door to room 701 was open somehow
shadows drifted in. Smoke of three strangers drew hard sticks from
inside their coats he struggled too late to rise from a vivid dream. One
of these intruders stayed by the door while the others advanced
through the curtains burst faint squibs of daylight. The blows fell hard
on his upper body or legs for variety a fly screwed up from the
bedhead.

We're here for your life, foreign dog.

He had feared this since summer last year the border checkpoint
often closed. With their valleys of silver trees in winter his mouth and
throat were unbearably dry one side of the border a continuation of
the other.

Somewhere in this frozen world a bone cracked loudly his
assailants were out for serious damage. They hadn't said who they
were but he guessed struggling furiously they wanted revenge for that
trouble on the other side his ribs ached. One blow flattened his nose
like dogs they snarled about their friend in hospital back home.

Soon you will die.

Pytor saw their leader advance heart racing across the carpet. His
face was streaming blood in the future the stranger said that border
traders from their side would deal with those from ours

only on theirs.

When they were done his cold stiff body would be returned as a
message

the beating intensified

Now you die.

The Strike

The merciless sticks rained down at ever shorter intervals voices in the empty blueness wondering whether he was dreaming familiar voices. The door opened unexpectedly his friends Vladimir and Dmitri were there flanked by hotel attendants the morning just begun. They faced down his assailants with cudgels on the other side of the planet night descending. The stand off ended abruptly the intruders went to the door and left shouting threats.

Vladimir coughed as he approached the bed splattered with blood the beaten man groaning. The floor uncle sighed repeatedly flies on the ceiling saying how terrible it was.

You're lucky we're here, brother.

The floor uncle left and Pytor's friends helped him to stand on sore legs faint sunlight slunk through the curtain. After a while he was able to pace the room from side to side wiping his bloodshot eyes. He tried first one leg and then the other cautiously they reckoned nothing broken. There was a sharp pain in the area of his left hip this morning they warned the streets dangerously icy.

We thought this might happen.

Only last night at dinner they'd discussed the trader from Suifen badly beaten in the streets of their town there were always going to be consequences. The cops did nothing to help even after his leg had to be amputated they handed him a flask of snake wine.

You need this.

The snake eased his pain eventually Vladimir said Pytor had offered to help his cousin Katya set up a shoe deal. Last night in the restaurant Vladmir was smashed chasing waitresses behind the bar and falling flat on his face a cassette deck poured out 80s pop. Pytor decided to keep his promise slapping his leather cap over his throbbing head floorboards squeaking.

One more for the road, brothers.

On a bright winter morning they descended past the third floor brothel's nude frescoes all night the piercing moans keeping him awake. Downstairs lobby latecomers refuelled with breakfast buffet porridge and pickled vegetables beyond the windows streets lay white and cold as metal. In the forecourt they saw ranks of donkey carts and yellow taxis embedded in ice the drivers' faces leathery. They left along the street of small shops people and languages thawed out the up and down day. After Dmitri departed on some business the two others got in a taxi the flask passed back and forth.

The border.

As Dmitri told the driver to rush them to the border station by the quickest route Pytor thought of Miss Wei at the Customs Bureau. Although he ached from his beating when gentle Miss Wei appeared in his mind the jerking taxi seemed to have no suspension. He often daydreamed about introducing this woman he fancied to his mother in their small house with the border always shutting they hadn't met for months now. His mother kept hinting he should settle down so a family could begin he imagined his sweetheart close beside him. She had darkly watchful but somehow teasing eyes each time crossing the border he couldn't wait to see her.

I never know when you're going to vanish.

At the station the train had already pulled in a cloud of bluely dust releasing a mass of their fellow border traders. As the sky was low hundreds streamed onto the frosty street of small hotels pulling red and white striped bags. While the morning passed in the speckled air women leaking dry blonde hair from wool hats hauled the heavy bags into bread vans.

The whole time Pytor stayed nervous looking around him violence ready to erupt at any moment. Excited groups of men with big coats talked loudly about going for a drink at the Far East Hotel birds floating with the wind. Amid the commotion they handed the flask between them and waited for Katya as usual few going the other way until there she was waving.

You guys must be blind.

She was Katya had left early that morning for the train in a snowstorm black pigs riding to the border. At such times her nose was florid red back home more people rode dog carts. Although the world wasn't breathing she ate a boiled egg before setting out her husband's feet warm and hairy. A square blue car sat abandoned frozen at the border she crossed twice a year as a buyer for her sister's shoe shop. As the train sped silently through white forests foreign notes folded in a bag around her neck all these small lined valleys.

You can't trust anyone on that side... they're all crooks.

Since last time they overcharged her for leather boots until cousin Vladimir promised to introduce his young friend as a translator. The friend was kind of handsome although his face had taken a real beating she likely wasn't his type.

We'll go straight there.

Because a freezing gale had got up they took a taxi all the way to the square locals guzzling soup noodles in little restaurants. The town centre was a cluttered citadel of shops where traders wrapped in fur hats and coats bought eggs at this early hour. She liked most the times her second husband came once or twice a year they stayed in the Far East Hotel shopping for electric steamers and kettles. After crossing the border screwing was more exciting she smiled with a full purse of exotic notes and coins.

How can they live in this place?

They felt the wind bite after leaving the taxi the entrance to the underground market was right there. They pushed aside the plastic curtain and entered tunnels dug thirty years ago old border tension flaring Katya saw familiar faces from the train. Beneath the city this labyrinth ran forever and ever cubicles and cubicles shoes and shoes and coats and coats and alarm clocks. The three of them descended floor after floor of new year decorations and plastic dummies with sad faces seeking the shoe kiosk. At last they approached a spotty teenager eating noodles under her dark wool hat red hairs extruding spikily Katya whispered

Bitch with the boots.

Pytor handled it calmly after a while Spotty became friendly and offered tea in tiny cups they sat down. Boxes of boots arrived within minutes and were tipped all over the floor the people on this side friendly enough.

As Pytor checked the boots with expert care his mind drifted back to his crush at the Customs Bureau. There was something about her different from the women back home expertly probing fur lined cavities. Although life on both sides of the border had similarities he used a lighter confirming the quality Miss Wei had this calm refined air. He didn't even know her first name after thorough inspection they agreed a price for the boots.

We'll take the lot.

She was Katya after Pytor shook on a deal they went back outside hawkers calling from stalls red with candied fruits stumbling through white border fog towards the usual café. To celebrate their good business she took a swig from Vladmir's flask a hungry yelp breaking loose the others cracked up.

Quick food, guys, I'm damn starving.

They climbed the rickety external staircase for cheap drinks in the air the second floor Hungry Wolf café was raucous voices reverberated amid warm smells of sausage liver and black pudding. As usual the long queue of familiar faces ran across time Suifen beer powerful enough that Katya soon spotted him.

There's your mate Dmitri.

The queue advanced slowly through the late morning past an artillery of beer taps towards the food counter. Almost everyone here was from their side jostling for space sausages sour cabbage and fried potatoes the floor tiles became slippery. After filling their trays they took a table on the far side of the room Vladimir was singing a duet with the plump waitress from last night.

The stodgy food wasn't much to celebrate they came here for the company and low prices. They sat down immediately everyone starting to discuss Pytor's beating that morning a caged bird squawked amid damp coats and hats.

The Strike

You're crazy to stay now, brother.

Pytor said this time the damn border had been shut for nearly a week

his boss going mad.

Their business was on hold over there with the strike on stuck at this stinking border guest house.

No one told them the real story even if you spoke the language

there were things you didn't ask.

At least the authorities here were quick to deal with any sort of trouble

back home

no one took charge.

You should be careful.

Pytor told them he'd been coming here for years shovelling down the heavy food they shouldn't be intimidated by those thugs.

There was still money to be made from the border toasting each other with snake from time to time

flareups inevitable.

That didn't frighten him even though he'd been badly beaten no point scarpering

they refilled their glasses.

Keep your head on, brother.

They stayed drinking in time and space the flimsy door slammed shut and open. As he drank Pytor watched Vladimir dance with the dumpy young waitress behind the counter plates shifting. Katya's body bulged bounteously into his after crossing the border there was more comradeship. People kept buying him beers somehow life seemed less urgent over here. He and Katya smooched in timeless fashion the universe unravelling.

Although too lazy to stir the desire to see shy Miss Wei eventually broke through from deep outside the moon already rising. He'd been thinking about her ever since his beating Katya approaching half drunk.

The Strike

Where are you going handsome? I'll miss you.

He kissed Katya goodbye and slipped outside inside his black wool coat this late winter afternoon closing in mean as night staggering along Zhongshan Road glancing at doorways. This sense of being followed stayed with him all the way to the stone customs building on Station Road few stars visible.

It's you again.

She was Wei Jiaying this afternoon Bureau Manager Wen had left early for an appointment with his mistress. She supposed she was lucky to have a relaxed workplace compared with her classmates in companies this day nearing an end. The last pot of barley tea was brewing when the plastic door curtain parted loud shout ice flakes gusting in.

You.

Quite shocked by the bruising around his head she rose abruptly a map rolled off her desk taking the teapot with it.

She must have cried out in surprise her younger colleague Sun Ling looked oddly at her. Jiaying guessed that she was red all over her plain white shirt splashes of barley tea.

What the hell happened to you?

She was embarrassed for him to find her here today left over cardboard lunch boxes of rice and fish stinking out the office carelessly he just smiled.

How are things on the other side?

Her job was to deal with border traders every week on the wall behind her desk a bright ski resort poster. Sometimes she wondered why they still bothered to come here as their bureau had little to offer them luckily the teapot hadn't broken. Since school she'd admired their capacity to take any hardship as Sun Ling fetched a mop these days their economy in a bad way.

You've still never been to my side have you?

Despite half a lifetime working at the customs bureau she admitted her skirt was a little wet.

The Strike

Was the landscape beautiful there she asked with valleys of silver trees

in her mind they said it was.

He joked perhaps his homeland was like a handsome but cold lover she laughed immediately

adding water to the strong barley tea.

You would love our food though.

She thought sadly that her husband Junjie was prejudiced when it came to food Sun Ling swirled the mop under her feet. He always maintained that foreign devils ate unhealthily the mop head matted with hairs.

There's a restaurant not far from here.

He looked at her with special intent a clock somewhere striking four.

Manager Wen is away this afternoon.

She assumed the invitation to be for Bureau Manager Wen as well but he said just the two of them since her marriage

never eating out with another man.

She realised Junjie would be home soon because it was Thursday Sun Ling seemed to sense her doubts.

It's not far.

On impulse and without explanation to Sun Ling she left with him as they hurried through darkening streets the wind whistled shrilly. The trader praised her language skills so fluently she supposed soon it would be night.

So this is where you all hang out. There are so many of you here!

Down in the basement on Zhongshan Road was a crush of foreigners who looked like Pytor on every table white candles burned fiercely. Murky air swirled thick above the bar it was hard for her to catch his rapidly spoken words. All around the noisy crowd was in full swing as they read the menu she felt nervous about where this moment might lead.

Beef soup.

The Strike

She dreaded removing her coat for some reason the bottled blonde waiter took their order. Although she and Junjie were reconciled she found these foreigners attractive despite the intensity in the air something just slipped out of her.

My husband works at the Bright Moon electricity plant.

He was Pytor tried not to feel disappointed as women like Miss Wei were seldom unattached a lobster red faced trader entered from the cold street wearing only a t-shirt. His fantasies had seemingly been only that as he listened to her speak of a son waiting at home the juke box playing a soppy ballad.

We've been married eight years now.

It turned out her name was Jiaying and she'd got a degree in her stiff green wool skirt and jacket appearing so mature. Her face was young and almost babyish though he wondered if she was married why they were having dinner.

So do you like working at the bureau?

She told him she loved helping border traders some days more exciting than others.

The pale skin of her neck disappeared inside her white shirt the beer easing his jaw ache.

Why have you never been across the border?

She was Wei Jiaying as a child she'd dreamed of being a diplomat although you needed connections the beer tasted strong. She wondered about the women in his life but didn't ask as he watched her the waiter brought their beef soup.

I've never had the chance yet.

She remembered about how Junjie's sister had married a furrier over there after finishing his soup instantly lighting up a cigarette. Her sister in law returned for a funeral five years later looking completely different although smoke gave her a headache she kept quiet. As sister in law chatted about her exciting life on the other side she felt a disturbing restlessness luckily her husband finally gave up.

In the past many women married rich men on the other side before

The Strike

going silent his smoker's voice was masculine. Now they mostly came the other way for economic reasons the waiter approached to work in dingy massage parlours east of Yanan Road.

You're lucky to have so much freedom.

Her husband would be at home by now cooking for their boy she felt slightly intoxicated. Junjie was trying to be a good father because she rarely drank these days her eyes glancing around the room in case there was someone familiar.

Is there anything here to see apart from timber?

She said yeah quickly

relieved to be back on home ground

plenty to visit.

Not far beyond Green Mirror Lake was the underground base where hundreds died

during the war everyone liked it there.

She said you could see what shit people would do to each other on their side

people hated those bastards as much as ever.

Wasn't that a long time ago?

She told him many from his side had died there too fighting the common enemy

in history.

The local people were forced to build the base afterwards they were all tortured

in the museum there was evidence.

How do you get there?

Take a bus she bubbled growing enthusiastic inside one hour you could be right down the tunnels.

Because of the cold at this time of year she warned him wear a warm coat.

There are photos you wouldn't believe what they were capable of gas and biological.

After the war ended she said those bastards wouldn't come out for several months

even eating human flesh.

Do you have time tomorrow?

Actually she'd also dreamed of starting a tourist business as a student there were many things he might find interesting. They made plans about where to go for the next half hour time really flew.

You're sure Manager Wen won't miss you?

Hosting visitors was her job she assured him glibly because of this annoying strike

they weren't busy this week.

She liked the idea of showing him all around the borderland he paid without fuss.

As they said goodbye outside she realised he'd been beaten up quite hard his breath touched her. The frozen world seemed to dissolve when their eyes met and he leaned in for a kiss in that moment the street light making his hair golden.

Until tomorrow.

He was Pytor as a taxi took him away down one narrow street a neon bar sign hung off at a strange angle his feelings tilted. He imagined introducing her to everyone back home on the other side of the border she would seem so exotic. Her small hand would hold his on market days riding his dog cart to town.

Here?

They pulled up by the hotel cream fringed curtains red uniformed doormen already approaching to open his door. Reaching for his wallet south of the border fares were cheap he noticed the three hulking figures in the lobby a fish tank.

Keep going.

He'd seen them almost too late from their rapid acceleration the driver hearing fear in his voice. They were his assailants from that morning the car screeched and lurched forward. As they'd no fear about returning they probably had friends at the hotel the lights very slow to change.

The Strike

Just keep driving, don't bloody stop.

They sped along the streets light falling on faces in the shadows of shuttered shops. He tried to think calmly what to do because it seemed they were serious after sundown there was really nowhere else to go.

The border.

The driver turned the car abruptly he thought how Jiaying had told him he could call her any time. He wondered what the hell she would say if he showed up at her place tonight could this damn car not go any faster. As they finally drew up outside the border station he remembered her husband in the harsh floodlights there was usually no parking here.

Stop, I'm getting out.

Inside the vast cold customs hall he still feared assailants might burst from out of nowhere the customs guards checking his passport. They waved him through with seconds to spare until the last train his footsteps echoed hastening towards the sign National Gateway. The border lay beyond lost in shadow he pressed on into a faraway world.

Safe return.

She was Jiaying was clearing up after her family's supper she couldn't decide what the hell had happened tonight. She kept imagining taking the border trader to the enemy base apparently when you looked across from on top you could see far into his country. The terrible vastness of snow ice cities streets flooded her imagination afterwards she might guide him down through secret tunnels. Suddenly she felt sick with nerves although she hadn't done anything wrong when she considered the boy charred onion was hard to remove from pots. Her son was reading a book with Junjie in bed she would have to tell this man she was busy. After the receptionist put her through to his room at the Far East Hotel the phone rang endlessly her heart raced. There was no one there it seemed in the end that he'd disappeared again across the border unknowable.

The Strike

13

That night he was Chen Yun with Little Xu at her uncle's home sunflower seed and peanut shells littering the floor. They'd knocked back snake wine for hours waiting for Zhou Anguo to show up the local station was broadcasting Boss Cui's daughter's wedding.

He was Chen Yun comfortable with Uncle Xu in this industrial sprawl these Suifen comrades had slaved for decades making railcars. This place felt just like his hometown everywhere you looked brick factories black coal working people smeared across the sky the rail tracks and warehouses where they brought up their kids.

We had hope once he told Uncle Xu when the miners came out they tried to grind us under.

Leaders don't give a damn about ordinary people.

He was Uncle Xu sloshed more snake wine in their glasses waiting for the police time seemed to be dragging. Annoyingly this troublemaker wouldn't shut up within the worn brown universe tree branches rattling ominously the wind outside.

They eat you up and then they spit you out.

He was Chen Yun before the pit closed often ate out with a gang of his fellow miners li peng zhou dawei talking loudly as hotpot soup bubbled with garlic and fishballs drinking snake wine hebin beer. Comradeship and smoke swirling above sticky plastic tables they talked loudly for hours red faced waiters running in and out with plates of lamb and tofu and cabbage.

These Suifen people were powerless to defend themselves on the television Boss Cui's daughter gyrating in her wedding dress for the

The Strike

cameras. He told Uncle Xu the story of their pit in the background
wedding guests flaunting themselves.

So much money wasted by officials on foreign study trips Uncle
Xu staring blankly at the pretty bride in her white dress.

Once after fifty died in a flood they sent in an investigation team
from the province
    leaders in evening dress sliding from fancy cars.

We had more equality before.

He was Uncle Xu hoped Officer Zhang would arrive soon despite
so much snake the wait difficult. Old Zhou had promised the arrest
would happen without incident this was a winter to forget. His wife
and daughter were hiding in the kitchen doors half-shut Xu Yue's help
couldn't be counted on.

The strike taught us the truth about who we are.

He was Chen Yun only after the fuse box on the wall crackled hot
had he learned the satisfaction of bringing people round during free
flowing nights like this. Most realised the truth after the first bodies
were brought up from the pit soot black and stiff the system had to
change. Of course he hadn't actually worked down there for years as
a union man Uncle Xu lit another cigarette.

You see he said shameless greed

Boss Cui toasting the wedding party on the television draining our
inheritance.

While politicians talked shit about new eras there were married
women selling their bodies
    the guests rose to toast the bride with their husbands' consent.

Why is it he asked Uncle Xu we are now the ghosts of this land
    no jobs no wages turning the sound to mute
    no futures.

Change must come.

That longing had built and built in his home town for decades their
lives crushed by powerful forces. Strangely after leaving his fury
burned itself out quickly like after a pit fire only desolation remained.

The Strike

The unrest had consumed much since arriving at Suifen he thought less about his wife and daughter.

You've got a fine town here.

The border trade must explain the more open atmosphere in Suifen Little Xu seemed strangely silent. How grateful he felt for all she'd done for him in difficult times love cut through fear.

Smile, Little Xu.

He couldn't figure out whether or not she truly was fond of him the television went to commercials. She'd acted sweet yesterday after he cooked noodles and came on to her for a local ski resort. Maybe they could try to start a business like that in the future money to be made from tourists.

Let's go sledging.

He imagined building a new life here together with her racing on through unmapped terrain. He would teach her the lesson of this summer no matter what our pasts we have the power to change hurtling into nothingness.

Hey where are you going?

Little Xu stood up suddenly with a faintly haunted look dust dancing in the lamp light. When she turned at the door tense faced he realised she must have washed her hair earlier while he was out for cigarettes.

I'm going to talk to Aunty.

She was Xu Yue went out the door unable to wait for Chen Yun's arrest in that suffocating room ash settling in slow grey flakes. What choice was there first unlocking the front door then looking for her boots in the cluttered corridor. The night was beyond if anyone asked questions she would just lie.

She stood in the doorway held by fear nameless beyond an empty field skull mud a short block of bare brown apartments. Wherever she looked there were television sets while time went on within uncovered windows. On the first floor there was one set on the second floor to the right two.

The Strike

She found herself picturing her birth mother deep in the night somewhere an apartment dim and closed to her. Her mother came here after her adopted son passed away early years ago hearing the news she hadn't known what to feel. One of these very apartments might be hers after all this time a lone car passing in the night she wondered if she was remembered.

Still she stood there on the fourth floor watching in adjacent windows two sets. She was unable to move in that same apartment they appeared to face different directions.

What are you doing?

Her aunt appeared shriveled in the shadows stiffening with resentment. She heard Aunty's guilty whisper pleading and false as usual Jiabao skulking in the kitchen.

Why should I stay?

You must stay said Aunty

a clutching shadow in the doorway. Without you here he might get suspicious laying hands on Xu Yue

to restrain her if he leaves what then.

As the night went on in her cold eyes there was desperation.

What's it got to do with me she wanted to know.

You must stay Aunty repeated

until they arrive her voice dropping to a bare whisper.

Otherwise he will suspect she said

pointing towards the room where Chen Yun and Uncle were talking even now he might.

What if he turns on us her fingers gripped Xu Yue and wouldn't let go

before they come.

What can we do if he turns violent because of Jiabao

you must go back.

For Jiabao's sake

for all our sakes.

Xu Yue was a good girl but Aunty never took her

as part of her family
the clock in the hall ticking.
What's that got to do with me Xu Yue asked detecting fear behind
her aunt's smile
grey fur boot lining warm.
She said I've only known him for a few days making her mean
aunt squirm
some creature long dead for this trim.
Yes of course you are innocent
Aunty reassured her in the corridor
what if we don't cooperate
if they start asking questions Little Xu
about five it got dark.
So what?
Xu Yue clearly saw fear in the woman's face made in history
you must think of our family.
We are family she said
her hands smoothing her sleeve
only wanting the best for you.
Raised voices came from the next room we love you.
Didn't we take you in here Aunty said
aren't you welcome to stay
as long as you like.
The whispering televisions were a reminder the cops would arrive
soon her aunt gripping her arm and not letting go.
OK.
She was Xu Yue pulled free of Aunty and returned to the room for
the rest of her life this mistake haunting her. They wondered where
she'd been in the unquiet night Cben Yun and Uncle on the sofa
smoking and drinking to numbness.
Where were you?
She glared through the smoke in her mind all men were creeps. He
should have told her he was in trouble with the cops her blouse

missing a button instead of hiding behind her. He would have no right
to blame her for what was going to happen knowing men the way she
did they kept coughing.

Nowhere.

At first when Uncle called her late afternoon she'd gone cold the
sun already setting because of Chen Yun's gentle ways. Confusion
grew as he said your friend's a criminal

he's done bad things

almost laughing out loud.

What the fuck are you saying?

She refused to listen to him at first but grew increasingly nervous
Chen gone briefly for cigarettes. Uncle's union boss Zhou Anguo then
came on the phone her heart raced

and spoke sharply.

The man's dangerous.

Zhou Anguo told her more softly no one would blame her if she
helped them

he might return any moment.

As Chen Yun was a criminal she could do their town a favour

that night

bring him to Uncle's house.

They both spelled out what she must do because of the shock her
body kept shaking. She didn't want to hurt Chen Yun but when they
mentioned cops watching their block right now a dark bird took flight
below the window.

After Chen Yun returned and she mentioned going to Uncle's house
that night his face so pleased he trod snow on the carpet. Over the
years as they hugged she'd learned how simple men often were.

You're sweet to me.

She didn't know why she was attracted to these unreliable types
instead of real men a thud of boots coming from the lane. When she
thought about the surprise waiting for Chen Yun a guilty smile played
around her lips the footsteps passing on by.

The Strike

Your hair smells soft.

He'd cooked noodles again in her kitchen that night a notorious womaniser Zhou Anguo claimed. It felt sweet afterwards when he massaged her back in the small room cigarette smoke making her head ache.

I'm not even pretty.

She was left wondering when her true love might appear now the footsteps in the lane approached Someone older maybe better as she listened tensely Chen Yun leaned over and raised his glass.

Happier?

He was Chen Yun sat by Little Xu secret doubts rising about whether union chief Zhou Anguo would be glad to see them. Still they had to see this night through as Little Xu clinked his glass tension in the room.

When will that Mr Zhou get here?

He was Uncle Xu tried to control his breathing as time crawled the police in the lane unable to find them. An arrest at your home stayed on file for a long time they would regret getting involved in the madness.

Soon now.

He looked sadly at his niece for three months his wife often asking her to go because of her lifestyle. He would never tell his brother what he suspected in a downturn it was true enough women suffered more.

Was that the door?

They stood abruptly the mutter of voices outside. The cops had finally located them in the entrance Uncle and Xu Yue collided awkwardly trying to get out.

Don't move.

Within moments Officer Zhang and two other police came in the sitting room Chen Yun struggling to get up. They grabbed him on television the Cui family had just left the banquet dishing out a few whacks with their sticks.

The Strike

What are you doing brothers?

You mustn't resist they said as Chen Yun had an arm free landing a punch with his right hand.

Because of that he suffered more punishment from Officer Zhang until futility hollowed him out the room shook with fierce roars.

Fuck it, you don't need to beat me brothers.

They dragged him into the corridor without ceremony the front door open. Uncle Xu wanted the troublemaker out of his house at this moment dead moon rising Chen Yun realized what must have happened.

Which are his boots?

Uncle got the boots while they held his arms at first he stayed silent. He wasn't going to acknowledge the family until Little Xu pushed screaming past Aunty in the kitchen plates smashing to the floor.

I'm sorry.

Now the storm burst as Aunty pleaded with Little Xu to go back in the kitchen he felt the dreams of their future stir painfully inside him.

You liar.

After they dragged him outside she was shouting too you cheat you criminal you lied to me

until the night blurred into night.

The police car left still shocked by her outburst Xu Yue took her hat and coat.

I'm going.

At that moment dead moon her uncle mumbled you don't have to go at this hour trying to do the right thing. She could stay in their house on this winter night

where could anyone even go.

You don't want me here.

She was dead to them from now on they would never be her family.

128

The Strike

She accused them of standing in her way from the beginning
cold moon ruling over the earth.

You brought this on yourself.

While Uncle tried to calm her Aunty said we have a reputation in
this town

you have shamed us.

Since coming here what kind of example have you been to our
daughter

with your messy way of living.

Why don't you go home she said you're the wrong sort to stay in
the city.

No wonder your real mother didn't want you.

Anger choked in the dead of this winter night Xu Yue ran out
wherever she could to get away from herself.

14

She was Old Yu's daughter feared flying through clouds trembling in faint light her mind sought meaning in the news received earlier. She should have had thoughts only for her father as the city spread like a frozen shadow beneath the windows another spine-rattling jolt.

Dongmei, no one told you I'm getting married?

After learning she must return because of Pa's stroke she called her high school sweetheart Wang Xin spontaneously clouds parted. This news of his coming wedding refused to settle as crew prepared the cabin for landing a memory of shared homework ached in her. All through their school years she and Wang Xin were sweethearts walking hand in hand in blue tracksuits above grainy fields smokeless chimneys. So much time had passed gliding above her birth city what right had she to feel disappointed white cloud again swallowing the wing. As she felt the plane lurch calls had thinned during the last few months a briefly glimpsed ice river scratched its way across the land.

Ladies and gentlemen, we are experiencing slight turbulence.

The small airport had hardly changed after all these years no one waiting in the carpark. Because the shuttle bus had just left a dead bird splattered across tarmac she approached the huddle of taxi drivers smoking in pale biting air the corpse hard to ignore.

I'm going to the Number Three People's Hospital.

The new airport expressway seemed empty they rolled on past dark mud frozen fields. Her mind drifted back to that day eight years ago now she left for a new job down south a city gang digging ditches. That was when everything started to change the car speeding although she never meant it to. Her employer arranged training the driver braking suddenly in an airport hotel. Many experts were flown in an ox blocking the road to deliver lectures on professional conduct. Her cohort of newbies were on their best behaviour in that environment the ox soon moved off and the car too. They were required by their managers to learn company values inscribed on plastic cards she saw a village of crumbling huts. Competing with team mates was the most difficult thing for her in the air around the village wafted a strong stench of fertilizer. She was seldom comfortable promoting herself especially remembering her shy father the driver put his foot down and blasted through a red light.

She recalled her former hopes for the future reluctantly the car entered the scruffy downtown. Even after three years she still hadn't developed the aggressive personality her company required by the old cinema a whole block demolished. There was something closed about her winter wind stiffening the flags in People's Square felt smaller than before. She wanted to be more open but a part of her was dead inside somehow her hometown had failed to win a share of the future. Whenever she returned she realised this place was still poor compared with down south the drivers swerved from lane to lane.

Still she kept trying to make her family proud south of the hospital their car cut across an intersection. With all her heart she wanted to do the right thing in this familiar place her father might have died by now.

The moment she heard about Pa's illness out of nowhere the driver stopped on the far side of the road from the hospital a sense of failure struck her.

She always tried not to think how her parents missed her entering the subway market once an air raid shelter. Weathered faces searched endlessly for bargains in this dim labyrinth she didn't know what was wrong with herself.

She emerged on the steps of Number Three Hospital visitors huddled smoking cigarettes. She climbed the steps with shortening breath a small kiosk sold cut flowers and wreaths.

There was a pharmacy in the lobby frail folks trying to live longer a sweeper beat a path back and forth with a bamboo broom. She knew that retirees in the town lived coughing and spluttering for the next new pill.

The overflowing elevator arrived after a long wait she tired of the crush. In this gloomy place it looked like noone even bothered to bring order choosing to take the stairs.

The hospital depressed her going up past radiology sinister clanking. The green painted fifth floor corridor resembled a miniature ward of sick people in chairs or beds trying not to look she went on. On a a stretcher an old fat man twitched tethered to myriad tubes in yellow and white striped pyjamas Dongmei's heart beat faster.

She read the list of patient names outside ward seven her mother briefly appeared. They held each other with tense affection Dongmei looking through the ward door. She saw a universe of metal bed frames and tubes surrounding her father the air chattered.

You talk to him. I was just going out.

When she approached her father scared at first hardly room to put a chair between the beds. His face had that familiar toothy smile of shy pleasure the door half open as if embarrassed to show feelings.

You're here.

She wasn't sure what to say as she sat on the edge of his bed a doctor in a blue gown stared brusquely. Somehow she'd been afraid that she might find something like death in his eyes clearing more space for her.

Sit with me, daughter.

Selflessly as others in the ward slept he made room for her in what looked like new black pyjamas. There was a pile of peel and shells scattered over the bedside locker she was afraid to show emotion the nurses should have cleaned up.

It's nothing, nothing.

She got up again to clear the locker he claimed it had been a minor stroke brushing rubbish into a small bin. She knew of course that several of Pa's family had gone before the age of sixty rummaging in her bag for the medicines.

I got cold, you see.

Family history mattered apparently the stroke happened on a bus with a small flourish she produced the medicine. It had taken a special visit to her hospital back home to get these pills the nurses might forbid him anyway the man in the next bed moaned softly.

So, Pa, what were you doing out in the cold?

She sensed evasion even now he hated talking about himself. As a young father he'd worked long hours without making any fuss squeezing her hand. Such modesty was not the style seeing him helpless with all these sick people she felt hollow. Her father's values weren't appreciated in this greedy new world the moans from the next bed grew disturbing. While time ran out he lay there attached to a catheter and other tubes they'd always had this unvoiced bond.

She had so many memories her pa smiling distantly almost more than back then. As a child he protected her nights needing to visit the outside toilet block the temperature often twenty or more below. She'd always feel nervous crouching above a yellow icicle-rimmed hole as the wind stirred papers Pa bravely whistling in dim corners. The walls and floor were deathly cold to the touch trying to keep balance as she shat or pissed he kept the dark at bay. She strained to hear him on the other side of the wall clouds of disappointment hung around his thin blue jacket. Afterwards they raced all the way to their smoky brick room ghosts chasing them.

Although she considered herself unsentimental their home by the sports ground was poor when seen through others' eyes swirling flakes among which she counted her own. At the same time who cared their hut didn't have an inside toilet for ten years the street latrine an extension of their house anyway smoke billowed from a food stand below. They'd cared for each other storing winter cabbages cycling home from school to pass time weekly visits to the works baths. She wanted to make him more comfortable arranging his medicines grimy birds perched on the windowsill.

The Strike

She couldn't accept she might lose him after a long day at the timber works he would return sweating and rub himself down with a towel. Even as a teenager she shared his bed sometimes while they read stories touching his chest for good luck. Now she felt helpless seeing that tube going inside her dry tongue a line between good and bad health. She couldn't follow where he might go in this life they always shared things. From now on they were both on their own in the bedside drawer he found an orange.

Eat this, Domgmei, and stop looking miserable.

He was Old Yu peeling an orange the future seemed simpler for now. His one worry although shuffling slippers echoed down tiled halls was something worse might still happen. While there was a positive side to his situation because he was still here they had the alternative to worry about. The extent of his ambition was to not cause more trouble the orange split in the hope of being forgiven. His wife Jiahui guessed where he'd been that day saying nothing in the doorway doctors laughed.

You just concentrate on getting better, Pa.

Old Yu drifted away from the ward and imagined himself lying in a grave Dongmei took over peeling the orange. He saw new generations chanting slogans walking around in a supermarket built above his tomb shards of winter sunlight stung his eyes. The slogans sounded empty but as a young man he had moved with the crowds unthinking orange peel dropped in his lap. Before he was gone he only wanted to visit that new supermarket once more with his wife fluorescent aisles humming.

What are you thinking, Pa?

The machine that kept him alive made a thin click as she handed over half an orange he wondered whether at this stage in her life she should be happier. He sucked the orange silently they watched a pigeon with a wounded wing limp along the window ledge.

Say goodbye to your Pa, Dongmei. We should go now.

Jiahui suddenly appeared laden with shopping the day was getting on. She and Dongmei smiled bravely as they said their goodbyes for the next few hours he would watch television. He wondered how many more times he'd walk all around that supermarket in the shuttered timber works the past slipping away.

You get a good rest, Pa.

They got a taxi home shopping spilling over the back seat for the first time Mrs Zhang told her daughter about the strike at Bright Moon.

It was very serious.

She explained to Dongmei how buses hadn't run along Zhongshan Road for several days

the snow piling up.

Hundreds demonstrating against the sale of the plant down south gray sky low Dongmei said

nothing reported.

What did it have to do with Pa?

Nothing her mother muttered angrily passing the snowy park where she and her friends exercised in winter

everyone already up early.

By the time the taxi stopped outside their yard her mother relating gossip about her tai qi group they picked up sweet potatoes and eggplants from the floor.

Aiya, if only your building had an elevator.

Upstairs in the kitchen Dongmei discovered that her mother had something on her mind packed with groceries a new fridge. The apartment which she helped them buy was far smarter than her own shared flat without discussion Mother boiling frozen dumplings.

Mother sighed as she told Dongmei that Old Grandma was fighting with her carers again now she was back they would chop broccoli.

Dongmei combed Mother's hair to relieve her stress the dumplings quickly bubbling to the top of the pot.

But when will we visit Father again?

Strangely her mother looked irritated as the sun sunk beyond the open kitchen window for some reason asking whether Dongmei was dating anyone.

Although Dongmei was a successful career woman her mother insisted on telling her

resistant knots of hair

there should be more to life than a tangle she couldn't smooth.

Dongmei remembered she had arranged to meet Wang Xin without telling Mother where she was going shadows grasped at them across the balcony.

Ma, I'll meet you tonight at the hospital.

Soon she was in a taxi running through white air stretched around buildings breathing in time. Silhouettes flickered through empty avenues one long ago summer she and Wang Xin hiking together in the War Martyr Hills.

Where are you now?

Wang Xin called her mobile back then so confident about their future falling as if nothing could interrupt it. He was waiting for her in a fast food restaurant noise pooling

in the background unspoken feelings.

I can't stay long.

The restaurant this sunny rainy afternoon was full of families amid a stream of muddy mop water time flowing backwards. Going in she stepped across a floor littered with chicken bones her classmate waved to her from a corner. The diners around him were mostly elderly people in padded coats drinking tea and children running between tables.

Where's your wife?

He reminded her he wasn't married yet absurdly

the tilt of his grin still caught her heart.

Apparently his fiancé was buying things for their new home in a shop somewhere east of Zhongshan Park from time to time

glancing at his phone.

They've opened a department store.

The Strike

As they ate fries he described the new shop just opened
less than fifty years ago
their city barely a village.

The shop had five floors in recent years his gut rapidly spreading
full of elegant desks cabinets and sofas
his fiancee selecting curtains.

At weekends the place packed and a canteen on the third floor
already looking like rain.

He kept talking perhaps to hide awkwardness she couldn't admit
she still had feelings for him.

You're invited to the wedding.

She said at once she couldn't make it in the old days such a
conversation as this wafting chicken steam
never anticipated.

He asked about Father's illness because they always got on a child
was crying in the play area.

She really couldn't believe that he would marry someone else as
their families were close under dull lights truth drifting.

I don't know what your bride looks like.

There was a photo inside his wallet she had a rising feeling she
didn't quite exist. His fiancé looked tall like many other local beauties
on paper the world refusing to make sense. She couldn't think why
Wang Xin should choose her out of everyone in their city this woman
would grow old with him

She's far too good for you.

He was Wang Xin wouldn't examine his feelings more than
necessary the salty fries kept his mouth busy. He needed a woman
who was fun as well as smart even at school Dongmei already
serious. He admired his former classmate's success working for a
foreign company down south the competition tougher sky hotter. But
his fiancée Lili was an internet model who did things no one had to
make him happy he finished his coffee.

Shall we go?

The Strike

She had always been more like a sister anyway after they left the restaurant embracing slightly too long a bus approached. These melancholy feelings were enjoyable in a way he thought they underlined the serious choice he'd made as the bus stopped. He'd never heard about Dongmei having a boyfriend although she'd been gone a long time her arms didn't quite close around his waist time slipping. They parted outside the restaurant a dog whined mournfully and shuffled off.

Let's stay in touch.

She was Dongmei wandering blindly through backstreets where they'd walked together years ago a few men repairing shoes before an old yellow house with iron railings. All her school days she'd slaved under the grimy lintels foreign carvings staring down until nine at night. Exam after exam since there was no money to repair these old houses doing it all for her pa. Studying until she was too tired to keep her eyes open a minute longer the results posted on the wall of the school corridor.

Don't do it, don't do it.

She was passing in the white air a man came bursting from a small shop with dusty packets of cigarettes behind the thick windows a long time ago she'd bought school stationery there clutching a struggling pigeon by the foot.

I don't want it, I don't want it.

The pigeon fell on the steps with a dull thud she watched as the man knelt a woman laughing in the doorway and wrung its neck with his back to her until it was lifeless she walked on.

She reached their old school in a daze years and years already passed. In the school yard a group of students were exercising on the same parallel bars their class once navigated under a teacher's watchful eye she peered through the gate. Back then they were keen on competing to see could go fastest from end to end the library looking new. Their principal urged them toward a fulfilling future in the science labs opposite a woman in a white coat writing a formula on a whiteboard. She and Wang Xin always had exams to think about day after day with family support staying near the top of their class. Their singlemindedness was chilling to think about for so long never naturally brilliant. They worked all the time as if they were mad she thought what was the point walking on fossilised leaves and grass under frost.

At last she reached Union Park just beyond the school gates her heart was in chaos. She would eat lunch there in summer the park busy. Many of her school friends had somehow found time for dates with the sudden sunny weather all kinds of people out. As for herself she'd felt above all entering the kids' rides enclosure her duty to make her pa happy a few gentle roundabouts and wheels turning. Those golden years were sacrificed for him a woman in a black wind cheater jogging backwards around the lake although little good had it done them. By now she should have been further on with life's main business of family beyond the frozen pond two mothers pushing small boys back and forth. She wasn't getting younger although she preferred to keep a steady course before it was too late she should turn back.

As she passed the kids' rides small monkeys and pig chairs swinging for a second time she noticed an old man asleep in a wheelchair. She watched him sat there silently a young girl gripping the monkey's ears covered by a blanket. Although the sun continued to shine gently on his distinguished head of gray hair actually he wasn't really old at all with his lids drawn she felt a terrible pang thinking about death how soon they would visit Grandma.

The Strike

15

She was Mrs Gang picking her way along slippery Shancheng Road stone huts huddled all the way to the mountain. Since her husband was laid off cabs massed on the streets she'd been a carer for old Mrs Wang. She remembered the air was filthy today to buy toilet paper unwinding down the middle of her world. Breakfast cafés swirled with soupy steam her lungs raw behind metal shutters. Because she was late she decided not to stop yellow icicles bristling from the underside of the public toilet.

She tapped on the newspaper lined window of Mrs Wang's hut this morning carrying a taint of charcoal. After that she went to the iron gate where a long stick rested the dog was aggressive. Sometimes it sprang up barking as she let herself into the small yard an hour late foreseeing Mrs Wang's sarcastic remarks. A greeting on her lips she went in cautiously the stick wearing a black wool hat.

Are you there Mrs Wang?

She was Wang Mingxia now and forever on the worn kang in the lotus position. Bedbound because of her feet life was tough. No matter how bitterly she complained to her carers dusty plants were still left on the television set. Last week she had been giving suggestions that was all about the correct way to remove grime from inside a toilet bowl Mrs Gu stormed out. Her daughter in law was angry on the telephone because it was getting harder to find domestic helpers her son married badly.

You should try and treat them like human beings, Ma.

She refused to listen unlike years ago carers were not needy enough. She always told her gentle son to pick the ones with a hungry air birds scratching on the roof as they carried out her chamber pot. Young people were too soft they rustled above her and wouldn't take advice although once she'd been a leader whose word decided things. She'd learned the meaning of discipline as town education chief nowadays so much food in the shops.

She heard her last remaining carer Mrs Gang at the window followed by the dog's bark struggling to control her temper. Mrs Gang was an hour late but needing her help to enact her secret plan she plumped the pillows.

I thought you'd gone out.

Mrs Gang's head appeared round the door with difficulty Mrs Wang smiled at the small joke. She found it ironic Mrs Gang made her remark this morning of all mornings snow packed on the window ledges.

The hamper from the government arrived.

Once a town Education Minister Mrs Wang was sent a hamper of groceries every month

Mrs Gang produced a six pack of coke.

Take that for your grandson she told her carer

there should also be packs of her favourite sugarless biscuits.

You know I can't have a damn thing with sugar.

Although the weather unfortunately looked bad today Mrs Gang's goodwill was necessary for the sake of implementing her secret plan. The purpose of the gift was to show that Mrs Gang was seen as a human being with effort she forced another thin smile.

Are the roads bad today?

Years ago as a minister her tough questioning filled prisons with a truculent stomach rumble reclining on her cushions. Because of her former influence it was frustrating she must do things in an underhand way she and her husband mattered once. After they decided something important they would get on the phone to the mayor without delay she coughed. Her husband was a force of nature slapping his fist on the table even the party secretary wouldn't cross him. They worked so hard when their children were small having the use of a government car. At six am they usually went for breakfast with the mayor leaving their son at home alone her husband liked to start the day with hot soy milk. She knew that her daughter-in-law blamed her for not helping them early on the daft woman understood nothing. Back then the political environment too dangerous to take risks after three years of exile in the countryside her husband's health never recovered. Three of her own toes had died wrapped in a thick flowery sock the world shrunk and withered.

As senior cadres they were easy targets following her illness last autumn she hadn't been outside. Now she hoped Mrs Gang might be cooperative regarding her secret plan the room's stale air suffocating.

You remember my daughter in law will visit today?

The plan came to her yesterday afternoon the gas bill arriving. It seemed reasonable despite Mrs Gang's sure opposition she herself would go to pay what was due. The post office was only ten minutes from her house as she remembered you took a left then kept straight on. All last night she had planned the route in her mind snow drifts the whole way assuming it still existed. For hours she imagined herself being wheeled most elegantly along the familiar street a ripple of applause. It would be better if the sun shone although there was no guarantee most of the old neighbours probably moved away. How fine the stonework of the post office built forty years ago during her time as education chief her husband running construction. Very optimistic it made her feel to see herself ride past it under a white sky her hair nicely washed and combed. She last went there about five years ago to post a letter to an old colleague in the capital many cultured people. The colleague hadn't replied to this day she thought she would ask the post office staff about it.

Are the streets slippery would you say, Mrs Gang?

She knew the importance of retaining an interest in life outside these four wall often strange and even alarming sounds. As a mental exercise she would often question her helper ignorant as she was about festivals or the trouble in Suifen disturbing developments. Now she discreetly inquired whether the council had gritted the smaller roads while disguising her motives Mrs Gang unpacked the hamper.

This whole plan depended on winning over her daughter in law a low fog settling all week. Slightly anxious despite herself she wondered what she should wear on her first outing in half a year long enough.

ii.

She was Mrs Zhang sat in a bus following the stubborn line of a mountain pass. At the weekend sister in law called this high up the windows frosted. On hearing the news about her carer she had little choice although this narrow winding road was perilous. You glimpsed lorries far below houses with frozen maise on their roofs dropping from sight as you waited for the inevitable collision.

Only a few months ago Grandma's last helper Mrs Du had walked out over accusations of lost pills the engine groaned. An earlier carer had complained to the council about bullying since Grandma bore grudges until she accused Mrs Piao of stealing grocery money.

Mrs Zhang sympathised with her mother in law's carers the bus braked sharply having suffered at the old woman's hands. Remembering the insults soaked up over the years she struggled to hide her feeling of injustice from Dongmei the valley fell sharply away. She knew Dongmei worried about her pa in her green coat the family resemblance was strong.

We're going so slowly, Ma.

Her mind returned to Old Yu in his hospital bed they once often made this journey. He'd not confessed yet where he went that fateful day somehow she knew. Back when they first met on the commune

143

she got this sense from him of inner chill the windows icing up. She was an army nurse while he worked on a construction project in that wilderness it got dark at four. He found heavy lifting difficult since he was from a privileged family there were endless meetings. She saw him seem to stare into the frozen ground sometimes they dug irrigation channels. After she helped him once when he was sick repairing his jacket to look like new they got engaged. Circumstances meant no chance of a ceremony in his army barracks they pushed two metal beds together.

Their family seemed complete after becoming pregnant with Dongmei at last she realized the depth of Old Yu's emotional damage. Many of their generation suffered similar hurt she thought turning to Dongmei a bit sadly you couldn't make someone love you.

Do you remember the way to Grandma's?

She was Dongmei scraping her fingernails across the glass in frosty circles that familiar route down the valley appearing. Back in the days as a town official Grandma traveled to the capital frequently her sharp tongue frightening Dongmei. Grandma never missed a chance to lament Dongmei's school grades however hard she tried apparently she resembled her mother.

Although she hadn't been back for years Dongmei vividly remembered the squat half courtyard where Grandma lived window frosting over surrounded with barbed wire. She would cling to her father's hand in those days at the thought of Grandma inside the bus braked sharply. When Grandpa was alive they used the whole house according to Pa many fatal accidents on this road. But her grandma once mighty was now powerless they finally eased into the garage.

Everyone out.

The hotpot restaurant by the bus garage leaking steamy vapours they waded across the icy slush river of the street. Jiahui dragged Dongmei through a crowd of frozen fish vendors that morning her thick wool purple hat pulled down over her ears. After buying sausage meat in a vacant lot they stopped at a shiny toilet so Mrs Zhang could relieve herself a box of tissues and a fee. Once she came out they took a taxi along snow piled streets drifting towards Mrs Wang's house the clouds stacked up like chimneys.

Since Dongmei's grandpa was gone now stuffed with relics of the past Grandma Wang occupied just a single room. After they tapped at the window Mrs Gang appeared gesturing with a stick from the chimney a little puff of white smoke. They threw down sausage meat for the dog to guzzle as an apology a box of oranges for Mrs Gang.

We know she can be difficult.

Mrs Gang was moved to receive so much appreciation this morning after the coke as well no point in holding grudges.

At her age, she's allowed to be.

Mrs Wang sat regally on the kang in the warm room they quickly removed their coats. A nest of checked blankets harboured Grandma's discreet chamber pot under her white wool skull cap her eyes beckoned Dongmei towards her.

You've got fat.

These were Mrs Wang's first words to her granddaughter after several years without much show of feeling on her side

they embraced.

After that the old woman listened with a thin face to news about Dongmei still on her own her daughter-in-law said

a job down south.

You look well, Grandma.

She was Mrs Wang remembered her plan saying her days dragged because her family rarely visited

on the road to recovery.

Since the gas bill was due she even thought they might all go for a little walk together if they didn't mind perhaps

the post office.

The winter sun shining through the sealed windows they could take her chair

to settle a gas bill.

The Strike

The roads are slippery today, Grandma.

Grandma anticipating this objection said a cold strip of light across her messy bed

most roads were gritted.

Day after day sitting there afraid to trouble her carers for months the outside world unseen.

She thought it would be agreeable to go with her granddaughter and daughter in law

treating her like she was already dead.

Grandma, you haven't been well recently.

Mrs Wang couldn't conceal how resentful she felt because the small hut smelled of old socks. Her family left her in the hands of her carers she said

she'd suffered so much nothing ever thrown out.

Although it was important to be on best behaviour somehow she heard herself complaining about dirty plants on the television.

Grandma, if you'd been a little more patient with Mrs Gu yesterday…

Mrs Wang retreating strategically asked Dongmei to find her album of photos from half a century ago marrying her husband Li Pengfei at City Hall. Although he'd stood strong for which his health paid the ultimate price years later she was left at the mercy of her ungrateful family.

Where is my son, why didn't he come?

No one wanted to let on about her son's stroke because she was upset they comforted her.

Dongmei told Grandma how dashing her grandfather was in the photos because of his beard

you could see dust caught in the frame.

The album showed the newly married couple wearing uniforms one day in history Mrs Wang's eyes welling up.

You were beautiful, Grandma.

She was Mrs Wang remembered ages ago after bitter suffering at the party's expense she and her husband Pengfei spent a year convalescing in the capital. Because of being revolutionary martyrs as the troubles were over they stayed in a beautiful courtyard house near the hospital. Since they both had health problems day and night four educated party members waited on them. A driver was event available to take them to Zhongshan Park on occasions they were not busy with more important officials.

Those were golden times during which they met so many interesting people never keeping in touch. At the end of the year they returned home as heroes the paper wrote a story about them. Only a few months afterwards her husband's heart failed leaving her alone for which she might never forgive him.

Your son will come next time.

Mrs Wang wiped away a small tear for her frostbitten feet she'd suffered enough. She said how she simply dreamed of going out with her granddaughter to pay a bill draft stirring withered flowers in a vase

that was all.

She didn't know when she might see her granddaughter again in this life

bloom soon faded.

I don't know how much longer I've got.

After that they agreed to take Mrs Wang outside on one of the coldest days of the year. While Mrs Gang looked for the bill they wrapped Mrs Wang in layers of cardigans. They bandaged her slight body in scarves and blankets like a white sheep's skull in the snow her face peeping out.

After pulling red cloth shoes over her socks Mrs Zhang and Dongmei lowered Mrs Wang from her kang onto a folded out wheelchair throne. They made her comfortable with cushions she thanked them humbly. She was Mrs Gang took the gas bill and insisted on coming that cold afternoon suspicious of what the old woman might say knowing her sly character beyond the narrow doorway.

147

The Strike

Isn't this exciting Grandma?

She was Wang Mingxia as they wheeled her out across the yard long white skies above. They pushed her through the gate for the first time in years Dongmei unchaining the dog. She sat up straight observing everything Dongmei followed with the dog sniffing hard ground. Her blankets felt warm around her body more familiar buildings left than she'd supposed. Her hands gripped the chair fearlessly they advanced past the concrete frozen public toilet. At the corner of Suifen Road a few men repaired bicycles as she progressed with her retinue smiling at her. She was happy to be outside today smoke rose behind wire fences their faces seeming almost warm in this frosty climate she supposed unlikely.

The chair spun on the ice suddenly she remembered a grander procession long ago. Because the defence minister was visiting their small border town as chair of the reception committee banners she rode with him in the black Hongqi. There were fewer cars then she accompanied the minister waving at schoolchildren with flags distributed by her office. That day she set out at five to supervise the military parade her children were left in the care of Aunty Wen. The minister was an imposing man after introductions she took them to the war martyrs' park built by her husband. They climbed on the plinth when she drew attention to her husband's work he said Bureau Chief Zhang should be acknowledged for his service. After the usual border inspection they proceeded through excited crowds towards the old City Hall birds darted overhead. She would never forget the minister sat beside her at the official banquet bird's nest soup served.

Mayor Wen and all the old team were still alive back then in fiery meetings debating orders from Central. They kept the town going through one political movement after another the leadership team strong allies. Unexpectedly her eyes misted up seeing the Customs Bureau opened by her husband loom in the distance horizon dim now. Such a strong man she thought about that shocking day he came home in a dark mood the chair hit a bump going straight for the gun in his desk drawer.

As he sat there with a grim expression they nearly spilled her in the road she asked alarmed what was wrong. Eventually he told her during foundation work for the new primary school on Changan Road a nervous pain in her head they'd uncovered a mass war grave. When he described those bodies interred there for years her back felt a little sore. Although regaining his composure the following Sunday he shot two workers guilty of counterrevolutionary activity.

That was the kind of emotional man her beloved Pengfei was each summer their team of top leaders had a picnic in the countryside. They were driven there by Mayor Wen himself afterwards boxes of pears being handed out. Uncle Wen was driven to his grave early by the crimes of a small gang of traitors just like her husband the roads in a bad state. She cursed their fate seeing the way her daughter in law spoke to her the golden years felt irretrievably lost.

Your arm's coming out again, Grandma.

She was Mrs Zhang although Dongmei offered to push her mother in law on the ice responsibility was still hers. Much as she'd always longed to give the old woman a piece of her mind years ago the opportunity slipped away. What was the point now for dear Old Yu's sake bearing all slights. She remembered when Dongmei was small the mayor presented Grandma with a television at that time little in the way of entertainment. Grandma gifted this rare thing to a colleague although Old Yu claimed not to mind the person didn't even have children. She felt her eyes glisten on this slippery path an endless struggle for acceptance. Although she tried her best there were those who wouldn't recognise her later she would have to lie down for a while.

Nearly there, Grandma.

She was Dongmei when she thought about it her whole life white air smothered the mountains. She'd never imagined Father would get ill so suddenly the injustice of it killed her. All her dreams of seeing him happy in his old age and now a small florist preparing a delivery.

The Strike

Such was life she supposed from generation to generation a dog's piss stained the snow yellow. Since years ago her father was left to care for his sisters until last week his collapse on a bus everything came around. Grandma's generation made history while her feet ached from cold. They stopped the wheelchair on top of all that they should find a new carer for Grandma's snowy face.

Here, here.

She was Wang Mingxia after they wiped snow off her face she felt better. She knew little of current policies around the post office these solid sidewalks were a tribute to the efforts of the past. By now her granddaughter taking over the chair she felt there was nothing about life she hadn't experienced. Although old Uncle Wen and the others were long gone just as they'd always said she was tough. They couldn't have done anything differently although the younger generation didn't understand she took pride in outlasting her former enemies.

It was just when she thought of her husband that pain swelled up unbearably inside her chest a large bus approaching. While he was always proud of his strength on this ice-blacked road exile broke him. For the first time she admitted there was weakness in him after all without which she might never have loved him finally arriving at the steps of the post office.

16

That day she arrived in the city lights bleeding through space Xu Yue went straight to the theatre to find her big brother Chunsheng. He took her out for hotpot with his troupe joking and laughing the vast galaxy of the city overwhelming. After that she often stayed at the flat Chunsheng shared with his big boned love Ah Mi when the nights got too lonely traffic sighing outside.

She found it hard to adjust to this life time stretching ahead. Sometimes she packed a striped bag to go to the village after a fight with family Chunsheng telling her to stay put.

At her low point fired from the Happiness Bar Chunsheng introduced her to his friend at Jade Heaven the girls were like sisters. Later feeling bored during the afternoons he sorted another part-time job at the station theatre serving tea quickly and slowly. The theatre was warm when she drifted there afternoons watching Chunsheng strut the stage. She realised she should stop smoking as it wasn't healthy he lived with his stage and life partner A Mi.

What if my husband should return?

Beautiful A Mi was singing her heart out on stage the world swayed with white longing. Her high blue eyebrows arched like insect antennae her glove fluttering to the floor. Chunsheng dropped to his knees in another time far away mad with lust for the young bun seller's wife played by A Mi. Made up as a rich merchant blue face for carnal purposes he'd lured her to Grandma Yang's teahouse. His ear lingered for comic effect by the crotch of her yellow trouser suit laughter swept the dusty hall.

The Strike

Raise my head, listen to the moon.

A Mi shoved Chunsheng with dramatic exaggeration at times it was hard to believe she was thirty. Their performance was approaching a climax A Mi's warm smile and large breasts would make geese fall from the sky. Because the wind howled crazily at the door she grabbed him with a rotten cackle.

You are rich so your cock is bound to be a big one.

The audience was in an uproar as the horn player blew madly Chunsheng dancing around his lover.

He was Chunsheng in love with his partner A Mi ever since their first time moon rising in that white van parked outside the station theatre. Aged twelve between her strong dancer's thighs he'd learned everything. She was six years older waiting amid props in the white van to be driven back to her village. Although he'd never kissed before she was well connected in the profession with a famous uncle. There were no special schools in those days the performer's trade passed down generation by generation poverty deepening. Theatre was a family tradition he squeezed the mound at the top of her legs a rowdy hall.

Show me the way to the sea dragon's cave.

When he was young his singer father smoke stained skin with creases under his armpits took him along to shows in Suifen bathhouses and theaters. As Father stood nervously at the wings with gaps in his teeth he'd hang onto bony trouser legs trying to glimpse what was happening inside. He quickly learned love was the most popular subject of entertainments in male bathhouses performing before lines of sweaty grey buttocks being massaged. His father dark and bendy sang everywhere damp with steam and hot water while naked men got rubbed down on benches he blew for them. A shy village boy he was slightly awed by these flabby factory workers meaty pricks from the steam gritty apartments packed all around.

Although not making much compared even to farmers in their village they were quite respected as performers. His father's long time

152

stage partner Zhu Qingshu was married to a dwarf in twelve fords valley her performance style well received. Unable to accompany them into the men's baths with her daft falsetto voice she sang dirty songs in the public area outside.

According to local tradition as a man and woman played different roles while one sang the other danced or the one danced at the same time the other clowned about. The one huffed and the other teased as a matter of form the partnership had plentiful permutations. Every now and then they'd get a week at one of the smaller theaters rough heckling normal. On Sunday afternoons when his father sensed the mood receptive Chunsheng was brought on stage after much hype blowing his horn for a few minutes.

Because of limited musical ability while enjoying the scant applause his ambition was becoming an actor.

After a while he was able to stagger and fall in an amusing way wearing costumes from the repertoire. At home in the village he would practice his act while walking over hills and feeding chickens. He charmed older players with his youth the future stretching ahead empty and free.

My husband is an impulsive man.

His partner A Mi was from a similar background in those days her uncle called a superstar of the stage. At the age of sixteen she was already delighting audiences by faking acts of love in a bright red dress the applause explosive. Behind the scenes he'd never met anyone he admired as much as this older girl flowers in her hair laughing sweetly at him. Her bewitching smile drove men mad with troubling ease dancing like an immortal barefoot. Although some people whispered she was immoral whenever possible he watched her perform with her more famous uncle long wispy beard.

As the audience jeered Chunsheng snuck his hand inside her dusty stage pants the mildly drunk musician stroking a long slack string.

I'll give you pleasure you've never had before.

At last A Mi sank down onto the mat knees thrust high in the air blue smoke and her broad grin. Knowing what was expected he knelt in his baggy trousers the horn blew and dry humped her with lusty vigour the crowd rising.

Go on.

She was Xu Yue sat in the back row unnoticed the first performance was nearly over. On Saturday afternoons the split red leather sofas of the station theatre teemed with a younger crowd drinking beer time slowed. Through billowing shadows young girls tight blue jeans shuffled from seat to seat sunflower shells scattered everywhere fooling around

She was leaving Suifen this afternoon right to say goodbye to Chensheng and A Mi. In the village she and Chunsheng were from Xu Yue would spend weeks lonely stone valley waiting for her old friend to return from the city. She was so bored at home in those days local son Chunsheng still showed up from time to time teaching her several of his stage routines. Sometimes she spent whole days at his farmhouse two rooms and a barn with a cow dreaming of being in love his mother steaming sweetcorn.

A Mi was such a free spirit that Xu Yue found it impossible to hate her however tempting. A Mi cooked her favourite home town dishes quite often unsure what she was doing here. Noone was under the illusion she had any special talent smiling wistfully like smart ladies A Mi and Yu Wen.

There seemed to no choice but to leave the city each night dreaming of Chen Yun her bed soaked through with sweat. He usually cursed her bitterly as the stage emptied she lost sight of Chunsheng.

He was Chunsheng lighting a cigarette in the wings after the show his body hot. A Mi said she would go out smeared with makeup returning for the matinee.

Chunsheng stopped with theatre manager Lei Lei on his way to the dressing room slaps of congratulations shaking the sun further into tomorrow.

Any tips for me?

The Strike

Smart Lei Lei sat counting twenties and fifties at a table by the door an intrusive draft increasing her need to pee. She was relieved the theatre was finally open again after being shut during the strike a cleaner swept the floor. All that trouble from the cops because Chunsheng and A Mi added new dialogue to their act charcoal fumes drifting in from the street:

We are Suifen people, we like strong drink. We're the hardest workers in the land.

As long as we're between the sheets. Our women are the most bright.

For just a few pennies you have your delight. Our labourers are the most selfless.

They don't even get any wages.

Our factories are the most profitable.

The government makes a fortune by selling them off.

The cops cracked down because the theatre was popular with Bright Moon workers these leggings just not thick enough. The strike was over now thankfully their theater open again for the foreseeable extreme cold temperatures expected.

After the trouble you made?

Lei Lei reminded Chunsheng not to forget the afternoon matinee

a couple of orphans chasing about the hall.

She sold him a small flask of snake from a dusty kiosk bulging haphazardly with packets of noodles and sunflower seeds he stifled a yawn.

Get some rest.

He was Chunsheng usually elated after a performance he drank the snake wine from a paper cup. In recent weeks though not wiping blue makeup from his face tiredness clinging.

Spaces and confusion fell through his eyes naked in the dressing room the flask handed round the three of them. Grandpa Chen was applying cream around his grotty toes everything repeating itself.

Young Lin juggled plates as they lit smokes restlessness stirring.

155

The Strike

What's new, Grandpa.

Although once a dashing lead Grandpa Chen decrepit now played the clown in a corner sat a large spider. When Chunsheng asked Grandpa Chen whether he would visit his children across the mountains

hard to tell whether or not the spider was dead

the road might be blocked by snowfall.

Little Xu appeared around the door in her baggy coat night encroaching.

Hello monster.

In the dressing room mirror he saw himself a strange beast heavily made up she said she was leaving Suifen right now.

He gave her the flask amused by her dramatic emotional statement Young Lin snuck her a dirty glance.

What do you mean leaving?

She was vulnerable just like so many other village girls swigging straight from the flask life dangerous. Again and again youngsters showed up at their place wanting floor space for a few days or weeks temperatures plummeting. After Little Xu lost her job he introduced her to his friend at Jade Heaven the floor lightly dusted with powder. He didn't like to think what she did there night after night making a living not easy.

You come with me, little sister.

She was Xu Yue waited for Chunsheng to pull an overcoat over his stage costume icy draft entering. He was still wearing most of his make up on this bone freezing day they crossed the small car park. Their two room apartment was in a block behind the theatre Chen Yun saying

there was no damn heating right now.

Some residents hadn't paid their bills apparently they shouldn't cut off the heat during winter

money tight.

Where have you been this week?

The Strike

She smiled determined not to let slip anything about Chen Yun the stairs a waterfall of slush. Apart from Yu Wen she'd no friends to rely on either side of the door were festive banners. She watched him search for the key in his pockets after entering the flat its usual mess. The table was cluttered with greasy breakfast plates following Chensheng into the bedroom.

Sit there a moment, mei, while I shower.

He was Chunsheng dropping his costume on the floor Little Xu belonged to his heart's empire. He was loyal to A Mi but they weren't married even at their age easy for actors to find love. With so much emotion flooding their lives at the theatre his behaviour slipping.

What's wrong Mei?

So many village sisters came to the city to find a new life stooping to remove his socks. When they ran into trouble because of naivety ending up on his floor a mouldy slice of bread going bad. Back home Little Xu was a strange lonely girl hanging around his house for hours at a time A Mi said mould was a killer. She had nowhere to go after losing her bar job Jade Heaven always needed new faces.

Why cry?

Suddenly he wanted to make her laugh the sun was setting outside. Pulling his baggy pants above his waist right to his shoulders he loved A Mi seldom telling her. Little Xu laughed and laughed as his head disappeared up there in a funny voice saying

What can be so bad?

She was Xu Yue the flat felt so cold she always received sympathy not deserved. She wanted to tell her brother about Chen Yun but he wouldn't understand for a moment standing there stark naked.

I'm alright. Put that away!

As a final flourish Chunsheng flipped on to his hands and walked to the bathroom just like that she almost died of laughter. Chunsheng showering she sat on the bed unsuited to this world with troubled people like Chen Yun the shower splattering noisily. In her frequent nightmares she saw Chen Yun's angry face as the cops dragged him out the water pipes moaning. She couldn't forgive herself for messing everything up from the beginning

her mother should have been there for her.

Was it you I saw last night in my dream?

Chunsheng was caterwauling in the shower her head throbbed. She almost felt now she'd betrayed him getting involved with Chen Yun bright green wall paint glaring. Something was wrong with her once drunk Chunsheng resting his head in her lap. As long as Chunsheng was still alive in this world somehow it didn't matter being apart she took off her shoes and lay on his bed.

Was it you last night?

He was Chunsheng stood under the shower heater glowing warm water trickling down his back. He massaged himself with soapy fingers A Mi would be busy at the market. The world seemed smaller than before soap lost on the wet floor he'd no idea what he wanted. Little Xu sun earth moon needed him for some reason the water scalding hot although they had never done much.

Emerging wrapped in a towel Little Xu lay under the sheets his body comfortably heavy and warm. He drank snake from the flask by the bed when she started crying he put a hairy arm around her.

Do you need money Mei?

Her face changing like the sky as she wiped her tears his shoulders still wetly glistened. Her arm was so soft and white he couldn't help stroking it tenderly the afternoon lengthening.

I am always here for you Mei.

She was Xu Yue wanted to tell about Chen Yun when she felt his pulse the wind rattled the plastic curtains. She longed to confess how she felt trapped without anyone to advise her a big storm getting up. She would stay in the city for him do anything he needed no end to winter's fury.

You're my little sister.

She froze when his hand brushed her breast the green walls damp and blotchy. He'd never made a move on her before at the Happiness

The Strike

Bar so many admirers. He drank more moving closer fear sparked in the depths of her heart.

I will protect you.

She heard his words inside her a triumphant smile swelled the universe opening. They hugged across the line between dream and doing a photo of A Mi watching from a chair.

You can kiss me if you like.

They kissed near and far great fury outside clouds chased through the dark. His body trembled as emptiness pressed even trees unable to resist. She felt the towel slip below his stomach finally the storm striking. With new urgency he touched her back under her clothes she must be dreaming bra slipping off. They fell back on the bed curiously her hand exploring that cheeky gap between his hard buttocks there came a noise.

BZZZZZZZZZZZZZZZZZZZZZZZZZZZZZZZZZZZZZZZZZZZZZZZZZZ

Pa, what are you doing?

Hongshu bursting through the bedroom door Chunsheng and A Mi's only daughter in this life her horn raucous. Puffing hard the girl danced towards them in a yellow dress Chunsheng rolled off the bed.

Pa, it's time to go back to the theatre.

Hongshu naturally talented in a past life was selected as junior maid in a young prince's household. A musical breath of fresh air at the palace everyone said she would go far. When the prince's wife got jealous of her after just ten weeks she was pushed down a well.

Have you showered yet Pa?

She kept blowing Chunsheng and Xu Yue covering up with towels quickly as possible innocence feigned. Finally Chunsheng asked her to stop the noise in a short while

she must perform at the matinee

demanding Saturday crowd.

Just wait for me downstairs, alright?

Hongshu smiled cheekily claiming she was playing families with her friend Little Lin

The Strike

they were getting married.

She took after her parents for her willfulness the towels too small. The matinee began at two thirty she reminded her father

skipping naughtily through the door don't be late.

He fastened his trousers clumsily they pretended nothing happened. Wandering down they cuddled in the carpark for a long time she wouldn't wash her face where he kissed her. He asked her whether she would stay for the performance coolly

she said no going to the village.

See you later, maybe.

She was Xu Yue wandered away with a smile in dreams leaving today proof finally she was lovable. For a moment she remembered that boy who proposed to her once on the way home from school the sun setting behind the mountain. He usually stayed metres behind following her home for several days in a row shy too. One day though stopping in a bush to piss with a bunch of flowers he darted forward. The flowers were common valley weeds funny yellow flowers when he appeared throwing them down with a scream of disgust running away. Only a few weeks later the boy died in her nightmares she would see the smashed car and the tree. She could never forget that first time anyone loved her although not going anywhere the bus was approaching.

The bus the bus.

Xu Yue wiped away a tear hard world memories never fading of that hospital twenty years ago. Her mother lived in the city now loving others perhaps the bus's brakes hissing as it stopped. A few men here had touched her soul as the doors opened trying not to think about Chen Yun. She was leaving but would return soon drying her eyes a wave of laughter from the theater.

How far are you going?

She was A Mi back from the shops meeting friends the matinee already started. On stage Grandpa Chen told lewd jokes after seeing Little Xu's tearful face in the audience earlier deciding to give them

160

space. Chunsheng was thumping the electric keyboard in the orchestra pit one string player snoring loudly. While the show unraveled A Mi placed her shopping bags between her legs roars of laughter. As there was still plenty of time she stretched out on the dusty seat thinking about what they might eat later the noise growing.

Finally Old Chen finished his act with a big roll of drums little Hongshu came on stage her father clapping. She blew and blew applause blew and blew thin little cheeks and plain hair several people standing up the wet universe outside.

17

When Dongmei's family walked through white air to Zhang Shan's first wedding fifteen years ago it took them a whole morning. Today on the occasion of his second wedding because her cousin Lin Mu had hired a Santana after twenty minutes they passed the river where they once stopped to enjoy apples. Lin Mu in the driver's seat said they must leave straight after lunch today a holiday

his family needed him back by four.

Dongmei and her cousin had been close since childhood his wife keeping him on a short rein.

Although packing a paunch he still had that boyish humour which attracted many girlfriends before his marriage smoking cigarette after cigarette.

Dongmei sat in the back beside Aunty coughing in an elegant dark overcoat her son was flawed but adorable. Uncle had the front passenger seat fighting his craving after a lifetime's smoking a deer startled at their car's approach. Aunty and Uncle still seemed to enjoy a closer relationship compared to Dongmei's own parents the river was a frozen needle.

About three kilometers before the village Dongmei saw the hill where generations of her mother's dead ancestors had been buried she felt strange since the middle of the last century. Mother left her home as a child promising her on the way back to visit Grandmother and Grandfather. Their precise resting place was known to few although their village relatives weren't seen much they kept in touch out of respect for history.

The Strike

She was Dongmei remembered well fifteen years ago weak squibs of winter sun walking to her village cousin Zhang Shan's first wedding. There was no bus that went all the way snowdrifts during her childhood. She clearly recalled her mother's account of the scandal as Zhang Shan's city bride already had a child by an unknown father they entered the village.

The village was just one street beyond Zhang Shan's house a steep drop to the valley. Since forests here were protected by the government until farmland was scarce and closely kept. In winter the village was snowed under for months stopping the car while life came more or less to a halt.

A long red string of firecrackers dangled from the gate Dongmei helped Aunty Zhang out of the car. A flapping Good Luck banner was tied to a pipe she straightened her skirt. Several young men sat on a bench lane outside the door a crisp spring morning.

They went inside Zhang Shan's house time seemed to flow backwards. The middle of three rooms was once again a bustle of three generations wedged in every corner chopped chicken and hams. They proceeded into the bedroom with muddy feet this early in the century about ten friends and family members waited. Cigarettes were thrown round for non-smokers sweets wrapped in colored paper everyone relaxed. Celebratory red paper was plastered through the afternoon ash scattering.

Old Grandmother invited Dongmei to sit down next to her whether or not they were truly related. In her late sixties the ancient woman's rotten eggplant face shone with simplicity like a young child her meaning hard to grasp.

She was Dongmei thinking how fifteen years earlier Zhang Shan's first wedding had been in this very room muddy prints everywhere. Seemingly he'd added little to his possessions in the world her eyes stung from cigarette smoke. She remembered how busy everyone was fifteen years ago hanging up firecrackers and red paper luckily she'd never smoked. She and Lin Mu accepted the job of making the marital bed secretly everyone hoped this would help Zhang Shan's bride to forget the man she loved before.

The two sides of the family had celebrated as one in the intervening years her social confidence deteriorating. As her father was only just home from hospital and her mother weak today an ancient cassette player blasting out pop.

The bedroom was so noisy they went outside the yard filling with acrid firecracker smoke. A horse snorted locked in a stall sadly Dongmei walked up and down remembering one magical childhood summer spent here. For years the village was special to her because of that summer the yard all churned up. Now she saw this place was poor somehow afraid as Lin Mu and Uncle discussed Zhang Shan's new bride.

She's ugly as an ox

said Lin Mu the only one of them to have met the bride from a neighbouring village

Well people should be suited to each other in his mild voice Uncle rarely spoke up.

After all that was the problem before.

She was Dongmei remembered even as a child wondering whether or not Zhang Shan's first wife Ding Hui would be happy firecrackers blasted the yard. Although kindly Shan had the misfortune to be known as the ugliest man in his village most girls wanted out. He was short and narrow chested with just three rooms his family owned one of the smallest village houses. Several village girls rejected him as a last resort the groom's father paying for a matchmaker. The matchmaker suggested city resident Ding Hui only because of her situation firecracker papers strewn in the lane like chaff. Her father was relieved to marry her off after giving birth out of wedlock a cat slunk along the lane.

People thought that Zhang Shan and Ding Hui were happy soon after the wedding her infant daughter joined them in the village. A family of three they lived together in Grandma's house apparently

The Strike

quite contently Dongmei's mother visiting about twice a year.

When she was fourteen or fifteen Dongmei stayed here for one whole summer their class conducting research on social issues. Dongmei chose to do hers about conditions in rural areas sleeping at Old Grandmother's hay barn. Everyone made a big fuss of her to this day she was able to nod off anywhere.

That summer was already three years after Zhang Shan's wedding Dongmei sensed his wife Ding Hui not really accepted by the villagers. Although Ding Hui smiled at Dongmei when they met at the well followed by a pack of dogs something sad about her.

While Ding Hui seemed glad at first to have her own home raised in the city she wasn't used to the horse snorting impatiently in the stall. Moreover her mother said the village women had no respect for her as she'd given birth outside marriage the horse kicked the wall. Had Zhang Shan been able to get her pregnant it might have been different after the first year for some reason the handsome creature seemed agitated.

Although her mother kept vague about the details the following winter Ding Hui was found to have taken a lover. Her mother hinted that Shan himself caught them making out through a window his feelings unimaginable. Her mother never said the other man's name at last the spring days were lengthening.

After that Ding Hui returned to live in the town once again her father felt disgraced. Several people said the woman worked on the street market in those days selling vegetables rejected by her family. She must have maintained contact with her former inlaws for years her market stall always stocked with fresh village produce.

One night Dongmei and her family met Ding Hui at a hotpot restaurant by chance her red hair and eyes gleamed. Dongmei nodded to Zhang Shan's former wife's eye in a nearby copse a bird stirred while her mother made a point of being friendly. That was Dongmei's last winter in Suifen before flying south to college a few months later her mother mentioned Ding Hui was dead.

The Strike

About eleven o'clock the bride and groom arrived from some neighbouring village in a minibus trailing red balloons Dongmei on tiptoe barely saw them. As was traditional the groom had been to fetch the bride from the house of her extended family foot slipping into a snow drift. Everyone rushed to greet them enthusiastically Dongmei started snapping with her mother's old phone. Dongmei admitted that the bride was not much to look at late thirties by appearances her sock soaked through. The bride had a wedge shaped body inside a black suit an alarmed look with wide lapels and red carnation.

Dongmei saw the mature Zhang Shan could no longer be called the ugliest man in the countryside most people aged quickly. He wore a brown suit perhaps suffering had given him better looks and a blue tie. His face was far nobler than she remembered in the snowbound field opposite the house stood a lone tree.

She watched the bride and groom make their way along the path towards the front door everyone hurling handfuls of rice. A string of firecrackers ignited at the second attempt little spittoons of smoke sent chickens scurrying.

At the door Zhang Shan knelt ceremonially the crowd cheering to lift his bashful bride over the threshold. His knees creaked because the yard lay open to the sun they weren't sure they would all squeeze in the house.

Everyone surrounded the bride and groom in the small room hardly enough space to play traditional wedding games.

A red envelope was hidden in the marital bed stuffed with money the bride searched until she found it.

Dongmei and Lin Mu were stuck outside the door standing on their toes hardy shoots poked upwards from the eaves. From the room they heard shouts all mixed together people's heads visible through the window.

For some reason Dongmei felt deeply sad fifteen years before watching Zhang Shan's first wedding take place in that very room.

The Strike

Just as today Zhang Shan lifted his bride over the threshold now the sun popping out from behind a cloud. Dongmei was small enough then to crawl between people's legs watching them search the bed for money. Sunlight touched the clean sheets she and her cousin laid down so carefully her heart soared. The bride Ding Hui looked beautiful in a traditional red wedding dress according to custom the groom wetting his unruly mop of hair down.

Old Grandmother lifted the red shawl from Ding Hui's face at a certain point on that summer day all the doors and windows were open. Ding Hui's soft voice sounded childlike as she spoke everyone was smoking. Old Grandmother could have blown her over she was so tiny when guests pressed around there was a warm smell of drink. Even with all the people wanting some piece of her a few straws were stuck to her backside.

There were many presents for Zhang Shan and Ding Hui to open as the first wedding for both parties back then Dongmei believed her turn would come. They nodded as they checked off black and white television radio chest of drawers and plastic buckets all standard gifts at that time she felt happy and excited.

Now Dongmei wondered whether Ding Hui's spirit was wishing her former husband well from her coat burst an unexpected spark of static. Did Ding Hui accept Zhang Shan's right to a new life on one hand or feel resentment on another her body tingled?

From time to time she saw how the top of Zhang Shan's head now resembled a bird's nest from the valley mist closing in. He sat on the bed going through this familiar ritual the sun would break through again later. Surely he couldn't help thinking how fifteen years had disappeared like a dream light thinning. Picturing the way Ding Hui smiled at him after she found the money in their bed shrinking hope. Remembering how he took her hand as they walked from the house talking about the future birds circled dimly.

The hopes of that day were gone fifteen years later Zhang Shan still lived in this simple house his elderly mother failing. He remained a poor farmer making the monthly trip to town summer after summer they couldn't save much. His former bride Ding Hui was laid to rest now Dongmei felt so sorry the party moving to the hall. She became tearful at the thought of Ding Hui forgotten Lin Mu couldn't help noticing smoke drifted back into the yard..

You okay?

She told him about her feelings silently her cousin put an arm round her neck

smoke rose from his cigarette.

The crowd emerged from the room amid a roar of conversation tables were set. Many greeted Dongmei enthusiastically after ten years recognising few of them. They praised her for making it down south she closed

when the conversation turned to boyfriends.

Black birds dropped like dead rocks through the misty sky the wedding party advanced towards the village hall. The village committee had supplied four large round tables ringed by circles of ill matched chairs the sun shining again.

Out of respect for their important city guests Old Grandmother joined their table near the door bracing cold air. Grandmother couldn't really eat anything because of her teeth beer starting to be downed in vast amounts. Aunty and Big Brother sat either side of Dongmei at their table beer bottles and packs of double happiness cigarettes piling up.

Within minutes a feast of chicken feet pig snouts fish heads flowed above their table the sun vanished and came out again. Several of the dishes made Dongmei feel squeamish to her core everyone dived in. She wouldn't consider the plump silkworms children gulped down so quickly Lin Mu slipped one onto her plate. Her cousin loved to play jokes on everyone to make them at ease old political graffiti still legible on the hall walls.

So how about this trouble at the electricity plant?

Their village relatives were highly curious about the strike at

The Strike

Bright Moon mouths full Dongmei found their accents hard to understand. They asked Lin Mu how the protestors had got away with it voices overlapping

these troubles were associated with her father's illness.

Somebody said that even if their wages weren't paid temporarily city folk always landed on their feet without realising it

she bit into the silkworm.

We don't have any wages here.

The bride and groom rounded the tables toasting their guests as was customary dead chickens kept arriving. As Dongmei didn't drink bai jiu these days she did her toast with a glass of beer the bride looked jollier now. Shan also appeared relaxed in a way he never had years earlier draining their glasses.

The couple then joined the table of unmarried males corralled in a far corner the elderly village teacher blue jacket was known as the professor. He muttered remarks they struggled to hear because of his missing teeth Dongmei's hope that this wise elder might somehow articulate her feelings swallowed.

While the bride and groom did the rounds the groom's sister was a plain broad shouldered woman in her late forties. Taking a microphone hanging from the concrete wall like a shower tap she began to sing hymns. Unfortunately she failed to hold the attention of the hall a few years ago a missionary came secretly to their village and converted her.

As they listened they faced the far side of the valley through a long window threads of sunlight fluttered in. The sunlight drifted above the smell of beer in the morning air Dongmei sat amid cut remains of animals. The light caught on the faces of aunts cousins and nephews and nieces she started to cry. It sprinkled a kindly gold in the hair of the bride and her pink blouse Aunty sang about the love of Jesus. Maybe she'd drank too much but Dongmei felt pained with unbearable sadness the sun emptying the room.

Many years ago the sun had also probed through a hall of people

The Strike

no escape. All those years ago the searching rays felt just like hope clouds parted. Her mother curly dark hair and her father would have thought decades of vibrant health before them valley trees pressed dark. Aunty never foresaw her son missing out on college she wiped away a tear after one bad score in his math exam.

The promise of the sun was false back then they had all welcomed Ding Hui as family. Not one person had mentioned her today she felt increasingly angry. Although Ding Hui made mistakes all those years ago she remembered how her parents were strong enough to walk to the village.

Straight after the wedding banquet Lin Mu was eager to leave the village all chickens stripped to their bones. The main festivities over his wife and child needed him at home hastily more beer pressed on them.

Zhang Shan urged them to stay longer but thanked them for coming as far as anyone could tell
the bride smiling.

They explained about their promise to visit family graves on the way back sun lurching lower in the sky. Dongmei remembered how close the two sides of the family were years ago the car pulling away. Time waited for no one as the car left noisy thronging and banging on the windows.

Lin Mu looked edgy because it was half past two his wife's impatience legendary. Since he was a family man more than anything else the fields and hedgerows sped by.

Three kilometres on they found the gates to the cornfield swinging off their hinges fingers and toes cold. Aunty and Uncle were sleepy after their big lunch the car gradually filled with farty flavours. Lin Mu and Dongmei set off alone across the field frozen with no suggestion of spring to come.

Lin Mu had last visited grandmother and grandfather's grave more than two years ago he claimed
work worse than ever.

He mentioned a computer course Bright Moon offered corn stubble rattling underfoot.

The future doesn't wait for anyone.

Grandmother and Grandfather were resting forever in the sheltered hollow just below the peak of the wooded hill hard to find. The hillside cemetery had been in use for most of the past century they occupied one of the better plots. Luckily Lin Mu knew where to crawl through bushes and sharp thorns to enter Dongmei snagged her coat on a thorn.

Dongmei tried to think of the last time she had visited this place with her parents on tomb sweeping day standing silently before the stone. After a pause Lin Mu produced two cigarettes putting one in each corner of his mouth inhuman cries lighting them. Very carefully placing them on the plinth large dark birds watched from the bushes as tribute. She would wonder all the way home whether or not their cigarettes were smouldering the afternoon rapidly drew in.

As they walked back down the darkening cornfield from out of nowhere Lin Mu revealed Zhang Shan's first wife Ding Hui was buried nearby.

She used to come here on tomb sweeping day.

Although Dongmei knew that Ding Hui had died in a city road accident several years ago this was a surprise. She'd always assumed this tragic woman to be buried in an urban cemetery under the circumstances her body went tense.

Her cousin said Zhang Shan insisted on her being interred near the village despite everything

she was his wife.

He even paid for the funeral.

Dongmei decided it was right to visit Ding Hui today Zhang Shan's first wife would need support. When Lin Mu realised she was serious although the afternoon was passing his old feelings for his cousin surfaced. Lin Mu knew the general location of the grave but they wandered for ages over the hill looking for it the sun sank lower. They found the marker stone finally in a ditch at the bottom of the hill snow piled up. Standing side by side at the edge of the field they read names dates followed by loving mother. It was strange after a while signs appeared that someone else had been here recently. The ground was swept around the stone greenery from the wood. A few words were scratched not quite legible in the dirt Dongmei rubbed her eyes.

Surely it was no coincidence she thought if someone came here today of all days the grave loose in the damp field like a decayed tooth. Most likely Zhang Shan himself visited his ancestors on his wedding morning as was customary taking the opportunity to call on Ding Hui. When the scandal of Zhang Shan's divorce broke during Dongmei's first year at college she was caught up with other things. She remembered the last time she saw Ding Hui that summer a lifetime ago they never really spoke. With her grey scarf covering her head Ding Hui was returning from the well lost in thought apparently it was getting late. Smiling at Dongmei in the white afternoon neither of them said anything.

Dongmei thought Zhang Shan had probably been here before starting his new life seeking her blessing. Or could there be someone else in the village who still cherished memories of her after all these years they moved away from the grave. She and Lin Mu went on discussing it in the late sunshine all the way to the car. It was impossible to say.

Talking with Harvey Thomlinson About His Invented Language Interview with Tantra Bensko

Interview first published on Experimental Writing website (2018).
One of the most ground breaking and important new developments in innovative fiction writing I feel comes from the new syntax created by writer and translator, Harvey Thomlinson. This new use of syntax is a method he's used for years to create a kind of idioglossia that shakes up the synapses of readers in a way that can deliver new perspectives on the world and the nature of reality. I was happy to be able to dialog with Harvey about this formally, which can be read below.

Excerpts of his unpublished novel have been published in magazines in journals in the UK, and now two are in Exclusive Magazine, with his commentary on them. http://exclusive3.weebly. com/flash-fiction.html I feel when this is published as a whole by some adventurous press ready to take the risk with a novel that is both experimental and dealing realistically with real world events in an engaged way, it will become one of the most analysed techniques in literary fiction. I feel linguists and psychologists, literary critics and professors will find this to be a stunning new revelation of possibility.

The Strike

Harvey is most known as the translator of Chinese novelist Murong's A Novel of Chengdu, which was a finalist for the 2009 Man Asia Literary Prize. Harvey also runs Make-Do Publishing, which presents some of the best contemporary writing in Asia. Here follows our discussion.

Tantra:

Your writing style is adventurous, particularly your sentence structures. People so easily take for granted the usual way of writing, grammatically, and experimental fiction has the opportunity to shake that up. One of the fascinating aspects of innovative writing is stretching our minds to think new ways, and language is intricately involved in how we think. I feel your use of syntax creates a new language, and it has been proven that people can less their chances of Alzheimer's if they speak two languages. Your work seems to me to have the ability to make our minds more agile and our experience of the world youthful and fresh.

Harvey, here are some quotes Clifford A. Pickover that I think speak to what you've accomplished. I'm curious to hear about your goals and methodology of making the new language structure. These relate to the Sapir-Whorf hypothesis, which says that language structure affects how we see the world.

Paul Kay, the linguist we discussed who is interested in color and language, agrees with me that language shapes the way we compartmentalize reality. There is a wealth of evidence showing that what people treat as the same or different depends on what languages they speak.' 22

Today, 438 languages have fewer than 50 speakers. {written in 2005} With each language gone, we may lose whatever knowledge and history were locked up in its stories and myths, along with the human consciousness embedded in its grammatical structure and vocabulary   33

If language and words do shape our thoughts and tickle our neuronal circuits in interesting ways, I sometimes wonder how a child would develop if reared using an invented language that was somehow optimized for mind-expansion, emotion, logic, or some other attribute. Perhaps our current language, which evolved chaotically through the millennia, may not be the most optimal language for thinking big thoughts or reasoning beyond the limits of our own intuition. 77

From Sex, Drugs, Einstein, and Elves: Sushi, Psychedelics, Parallel Universes, and the Quest for Transcendence by Clifford A. Pickover, Smart Publications, Petaluma California 2005

I see what you write as a kind of invented language that expands our minds.

Harvey:

The Strike uses a linguistic strategy which aims to subvert expectations about the correspondence between syntactic and semantic structures. Standard syntactic templates imply conceptual relations, such as sequence, or causality, and as Peter Kay says, these shape the way we 'compartmentalize reality.'

The goal of what I call existential syntax is really a traditional novelistic one of helping readers to feel the whole world of a novel and the meanings it contains.

Tantra

Can you describe the process when your sentence methodology first dawned on you, your first inklings of how it would work, your goals with it, and how it developed along the years?

The Strike

Harvey:

A few years ago in Mexico, I began to experiment with writing short pieces of a few paragraphs, and The Strike was my attempt to expand this approach into a novel-length work. The story is set in a rotting factory town in the far north-east of China, where the population protests after the government decides to sell the local electricity plant. The text works with purposeful combinations of phrases rather than anything like a Burroughs-style random cut-up. There was no single procedure, but the sentences often play with the semantic relations embedded within syntactic structures. For example, one line reads:

Although the world wasn't breathing she ate a boiled egg before setting forth her husband's feet were warm and hairy.

At first it seems to follow a familiar cause-and-effect pattern, but the semantic connections refuse to settle. The clauses coexist rather than resolving into a clear hierarchy, so the reader entertains several possible relations between the actions and images.
Something similar happens in another sentence:

Somehow she was afraid that she might see something like death in his eyes he cleared more space for her.

Here the expected psychological explanation is displaced by a small physical gesture, the father making space on the hospital bed. It still makes sense as part of the story, but the emotional meaning emerges indirectly through juxtaposition rather than explicit statement.

Tantra

Can you talk about your terminology existential syntax? Do you connect it with Existentialism?

Harvey:

Existential syntax is my term for a set of experiments that try to move beyond conventional syntax, which quietly shapes the way we perceive reality by encoding conceptual relations, especially temporal sequence and causality. Ordinary sentences tend to organise experience for us: one thing leads to another, causes precede effects, the past flows into the present and then into the future. What interested me was loosening that grammar a little, so that events, perceptions and memories can sit side by side in the same sentence without being forced into a neat explanatory chain.

It does not really connect with Existentialism on a theoretical level, except by analogy. Phenomenology, of which existentialism was one branch, was partly concerned with describing experience as directly as possible, without letting inherited concepts distort the description. In this sense, the idea of existential syntax is similar. The aim is not to abandon grammar, but to shift it slightly out of alignment so that the reader encounters a field of perceptions rather than a fully interpreted sequence of events.

Tantra:

Syntax in Experimental Literature: a Literary Linguistic Investigation a dissertation by Gary Thoms, written in 2008, breaks down Beckett's How It Is, among other things. This novel has a lot of similarities to yours in his particular systematic toying with syntax. Thoms refers to his arrangements of juxtaposed fragments within sentences as chunking. This is something you do in your own way. Thom says:

'This is characteristic of Beckett's attitude to writing: while he

177

believed that language was inadequate for true expression, he felt that
the goal of writing was not to free itself from language entirely, as with
Burroughs and Cage, but to misuse it with intent.'

You also have your way with words. The world has already
experienced Beckett's deliberate misuse of syntax, which plays with
time, and is said to be the voice of the eternal present. How would
you say your book moves the literary dialogue forward into new
ground?

Harvey:

The Strike makes use of what you call chunking, as well as other
Beckettian techniques such as deletion and elision. As with Beckett,
there is often more than one way of parsing a sentence. But the book
also tries to introduce new syntactic patterns.

Some people argue that experimental writing can never really get at
linguistic form, because readers will always fall back on standard
syntax to produce the most plausible reading. That is probably true up
to a point, but I wanted to see whether new templates could still be
felt, even within those limits.

In practice that meant working with sentence structures that resist
settling into a single hierarchy. One recurring device is what I call a
hinge sentence, where a phrase in the middle of the line can attach
both to what comes before and what follows, creating two centres of
gravity within the same sentence. At the same time there is an effort
to loosen the usual ordering of past, present and future: memories,
perceptions and imagined outcomes sit side by side in the same
syntactic space, so that time feels less like a sequence and more like
overlapping currents. The aim is not to abandon standard syntax, but
to let it flicker between several possible structures before settling, if it
settles at all.

The Strike
Tantra:

And where you see it moving next?

Harvey:

Experimental fiction sometimes seems to have stepped back from trying to shape the wider literary culture, which feels like a loss. For me, probing what lies behind language remains an essential part of the writer's task, not least because language plays such a large role in shaping how we experience reality.
At the same time, experimental writing cannot afford to become a closed or purely technical exercise. It needs to find forms that are alive for readers, that draw them in and offer a sense that something real is at stake. At its best, it should open up new ways of seeing and feeling, rather than simply demonstrating a set of techniques

Tantra Bensko is a bestselling author who won an Amazon gold medal for her novel, Glossolalia She also edits manuscripts and teaches fiction writing with UCLA Extension Writing Program and elsewhere.

The Strike

www.ingramcontent.com/pod-product-compliance
Lightning Source LLC
Chambersburg PA
CBHW060929120626
46557CB00003B/928